D0945534

The Rebellion of the Beasts

The Rebellion of the Beasts

Or, The Ass is Dead! Long Live the Ass!!!

Leigh Hunt

INTRODUCTION BY DOUGLAS A. ANDERSON

Published by WICKER PARK PRESS
CHICAGO
2004

Published in 2004 by
Wicker Park Press, Ltd.
1801 West Byron, Suite 1C
Chicago, Illinois 60613

© 2004 Wicker Park Press, Ltd.
Introduction © 2004 by Douglas A. Anderson

Printed in the United States of America

All rights reserved.
No part of this book may be reproduced in any form
without the express written permission of the publisher.

Library of Congress Cataloging-in-Publication Data
on file with the publisher.

"A man has no pre-eminence above a beast."
ECCLES, VII, XIX

INTRODUCTION

THE BASIC PLOT OF George Orwell's *Animal Farm* (1945) is well known: an uprising of farm animals to overthrow their oppressor, mankind, results in some of the animals being further oppressed by their animal rulers. This is also the plot of another aptly titled satirical novel, *The Rebellion of the Beasts*, published under a pseudonym 120 years before *Animal Farm*. Did Orwell know this earlier work, which viciously attacked the monarchy? Was he perhaps inspired by *The Rebellion of the Beasts* to write his own allegorical novel, an indictment of Soviet Communism?

There is no evidence to connect Orwell's work to *The Rebellion of the Beasts*. If he knew the book at all, there is no mention of it in any of his writings, now exhaustively studied and published in many volumes. There are a number of similarities between the books, some perhaps coincidental, like the seven "Rights of Brutes" that appear in the earlier book, and "The Seven Commandments" that appear in *Animal Farm*. But there is also much dissimilarity. As a close comparison and analysis is beyond the scope of this introduction, I leave it for readers to draw their own conclusions.

The Rebellion of the Beasts was first published in London in June, 1825. A scathing satire on the monarchy, the book was published anonymously because of the real possibility of prosecution. The text puts forward a number of red herrings on the question of authorship. The title page attributes it to "a late Fellow of St. John's College, Cambridge." The book itself is written as the first person account of one John Sprat, described in the text as a Cambridge student. The long dedication, ostensibly signed by a clergyman, John Pimplico, and addressed to "any Lord Chamberlain" (in effect, to any censor, for one of the duties of the Lord Chamberlain was the censorship of court entertainment, particularly stage plays), was perhaps designed to dull the attention of any censor looking at the book to such an extent that only a cursory glance might be paid to the text itself. Accordingly, in this reprint, the dedication has been placed at the end of the text.

The Rebellion of the Beasts was originally published with four crude engravings that have been omitted from this edition. Some copies of the first edition were issued with the engravings hand-colored. The number of copies originally printed is unknown, but it is likely to have been very few. A "second edition" (so marked on the title page) also appeared in 1825. In both editions, the word "Rebelllion" is thus misspelled on the title page. The publisher is listed as "J. & H. L. Hunt, Tavistock Street, Covent Garden." Here the story becomes quite interesting and complicated. J. & H. L. Hunt refers to John Hunt (1775–1848) and his son Henry Leigh Hunt, respectively the elder brother and nephew of James Henry Leigh Hunt (1784–1859), who is better known as Leigh Hunt, the well known poet, critic, and journalist. John Hunt had a long and close literary association with his brother Leigh. In 1808, they founded *The Examiner*, a weekly political and literary newspaper published on Sundays, with Leigh serving as the editor and John as the publisher. In 1812, they had run afoul of the British government by printing libelous remarks about the Prince Regent, and they both were prosecuted. Each of the brothers was sentenced to two years (1813–1815) in separate prisons. The incarceration was fairly gentle, for Leigh's family spent most of the time with him in an adjoining set of rooms, from which he was able to continue editing *The Examiner*.

In autumn 1821, Leigh Hunt sailed to Italy, where he founded a magazine, *The Liberal*, with Shelley and Byron. Shelley's death in July, 1822, left Hunt and his family stranded, and the magazine soon failed. Hunt did not return to England until September, 1825. In the interim, the editorship of *The Examiner* was taken over by Henry Leigh Hunt, John's son. The long separation brought about a bitter dispute between the two brothers, because John felt that Leigh had forfeited his editorship by remaining too long in Italy. At the same time, John Hunt had his own problems as the publisher of Lord Byron's lethal satire on George III, *The Vision of Judgement* (1822), and he was charged again with defaming royalty and bringing the monarchy into disrepute.

The Rebellion of the Beasts was published while Leigh Hunt was still in Italy, and unless the manuscript had been written before he left England, it would seem likely that there should be some account of it in Hunt's letters, but this does not appear to be the case. A long-expected edition of

Hunt's letters has not yet appeared. If the book is by Hunt, it would be his first novel. Otherwise, as things stand, his only novel is *Sir Ralph Esher* (1832).

As John Hunt was the publisher of *The Rebellion of the Beasts,* it is easy to see why the book got the attention it did in *The Examiner.* An advertisement in the 29 May 1825 issue announced the publication for the sixth of June, and another on the twelfth remarked that the book was "just published." A review signed "Q." appeared in the 19 June 1825 issue (no. 907). It is worth quoting in full:

> "Everybody has heard of the anecdote of the Turkish Vizier who, by his knowledge of the language of beasts, contrived to let his master know what an adept he had become in the art of ruining villages. This work is the production of a sage similarly gifted, who in consequence becomes acquainted with the spread of revolutionary notions among the beasts, and details the particulars of a political *bouleversement* of a most singular description. The thought is airy, and the execution eccentric; so much so indeed, that we give up in despair the attempt to

supply a due notion to it. Suffice it to say, that the satire of our philosopher is exceedingly devious, and that it zig-zags in its career like a flash of lightening [*sic*]. Sometimes it plays on ancient absurdities, not unfrequently on modern crudities; and, in short, seems no way scrupulous of making a hit in any direction in which a hit can be made. The progress of the Beastly Revolution, until the exaltation of the Ass, first to the dictatorship, and subsequently to sovereign sway, is narrated with much vivacity; but with a license almost as great as that of Rabelais, in reference to oddness and whimsicality. To conclude: the Author, whose vein of humour is very singular, appear[s] to have allowed his invention to freely follow it, sometimes indeed to rather out-of-the-way places, but seldom beyond the pale of legitimate satire. Query, has not the "late fellow" had in his eye the celebrated "History of Reynard the Fox?" for although after all extremely different, we cannot recollect another production to which this *jeu d'esprit* bears the slightest analogy. To say that it will amuse, is to say

every thing as times go; and that may be
said with safety." (p. 384)

The British Library attributes *The Rebellion of
the Beasts* to Leigh Hunt but questions the attribution. Luther A. Brewer noted this attribution in his
My Leigh Hunt Library (1932), including *The Rebellion of the Beasts* among Hunt's works, writing:
"the work is a satire well written. It contains many
passages of a Hunt flavor."

As the book is ascribed on the title page to a
"Late Fellow of St. John's College, Cambridge" it
seemed reasonable to inquire of the Library at St.
John's College to see if any further clues might be
found there. The library has three copies, two of
the first edition (one copy with colored plates), and
one copy of the second edition. The copy of the
first edition with colored plates is inscribed:
"Godfrey Higgins Esqr. Jnr. / from the Editor." I
am grateful to Jonathan Harrison of the St. John's
College Library for supplying me with a photocopy
of the inscription. When comparing it to Leigh
Hunt's handwriting from the same time period,
there seem to be as many differences as similarities.
With such a small writing sample it is impossible to
conclusively attribute the inscription to Hunt; and

whoever inscribed the book as its editor need not necessarily also have been its author. The recipient, however, was Godfrey Higgins (1773–1833), an alumnus of Trinity Hall, Cambridge, who is best remembered today for his eccentric studies in ancient religion, including *Anacalypsis: An Attempt to Draw Aside the Veil of the Saitic Isis; Or, An Inquiry into the Origin of Languages, Nations and Religions* (1836). Higgins clearly must have known the "editor" but little is known of Higgins's circle, which may or may not have included the Hunts.

In the end, as to the vexing question of authorship, Leigh Hunt remains a reasonable candidate and at present the only one. If John Hunt feared further prosecution from the Crown over the publication of *The Rebellion of the Beasts*, none came. The book seems barely to have been noticed.

The London Catalogue of Books (1839) still listed the book in print from Hunt, and it probably remained available until John Hunt's death in 1848. Even at that time, *The Rebellion of the Beasts* was at best little known. It then slipped completely into obscurity.

It does not diminish the literary reputation of George Orwell if we suggest that he might have found a model for *Animal Farm* in this obscure 1825 novel. Orwell's book has won acclaim for both its methodology and message. It is to be hoped that with this new edition, the first in nearly 180 years, *The Rebellion of the Beasts* will also receive the attention it deserves.

Douglas A. Anderson
July 2003

NOTE: Archaic spellings and constructions have been preserved for this edition.

CHAPTER I

MY NAME IS John Sprat. I am the son of a quaker who lived at Norwich, and who left me at the tender age of thirteen in a pair of fustian breeches and a broad-brim hat, to weep for the loss of the best of parents, and most pious of quakers; with nothing to console me, but a hundred thousand pounds in three per cents, and a whole room full of mortgages on all the gentlemen's estates in Norfolk. "Son," said he, in dying, "beware of the snares of Satan; and when thou art a great man, think that thou art of a humble quaker family, which will keep thee from pride. Thou wilt assuredly be a great man some day, for I dreamed on the night of thy birth, that thou wert born with a broad-brim hat of large dimensions, that covered all the counties of Norfolk and Suffolk; and that all the fustian of Norwich manufacture was expended to make thee a pair of breeches. This meaneth greatness. Thy mother, Jane, dreamed also, that all the Jack-asses in England came and presented thee with a crown, and styled thee the Liberator of Donkeys; and that after thy death, thou wast turned into a new constellation of the Heavenly Ass; which, though very obscure, meaneth also some great thing. Thou wilt assuredly be a great man. Feed the poor, turn out thy toes, help thy brethren, and twirl thy thumbs, as I ever have taught thee." So saying, my ever-to-be-lamented father embraced me tenderly, and, having arranged his night-cap, was quietly gathered to his fathers, haberdashers of Norwich. These things I like to reflect on: they are as the slave attending the Roman victor, in a triumph, exclaiming, "Remember that thou art a man!" for, since I have become of such amazing importance to the world, I fear I should become proud, were I not sometimes to think of my origin, and my good father.

Being much bent on knowledge, I put myself in the hands of a private tutor, to prepare myself for Cambridge, where I longed to shine in the literary world, though Cambridge was not a proper place for a quaker; but this step I was tempted to by my vanity. My tutor, who was a very learned man, carried me through all the intricacies of the middle verb of the Greeks, pointed out the Scylla and Charybdis of the optative and subjunctive mood, and made me understand to a nicety, the horrors of a solecism. In mathematics he did wonders also; and, by the aid of a+b, I could construct a pair of bellows, and define a thrashing machine. In optics, I knew by curves and triangles why I squinted; and, by trigonometry, I frequently took the altitude of the little house in the garden; so that Mr. Copper, my tutor, frequently assured me I should get into the first class of Trinity College, in the first year examinations; a glory which I thought more desirable than the fame of Lord Wellington; or the renown which posterity will undoubtedly bestow on Mr. Wordsworth, for having written Peter Bell and Betty Foy. How short-sighted are our hopes in this world! I lost the minor reward; but have gained instead of it a fame undying, immortal, and eternally encreasing in a geometrical proportion, almost as rapid as our system of taxation:—a fame which after my death will undoubtedly entitle me to be turned into the constellation of the Heavenly Ass.

When I first went to Cambridge, I met with obstacles sufficient to sink a less courageous mind, so often was I put out of sizings and commons by the great and learned men of Trinity College. The reverend, erudite, and pious senior dean would not let me eat any thing for three days because unwittingly I went to chapel in a black neckcloth; another time, he made me get by heart three books of "*Lucretius de Natura Rerum*," because I happened to sneeze in the midst of a fine anthem, the grand and sublime chorus of "the Frogs of Egypt;" and another time, he condemned me to attend fourteen divine services, and make two declamations in one week, because I came in somewhat late when the Reader had got as far as "*Pontius Pilate.*"—Thrice was I fined six and eight-pence by the proctors for putting my cap awry on my head; three weeks in my terms were taken away, because I wore gaiters; and I was reprimanded *ex-cathedra* by a bishop and eight seniors, because being pressed by a dose of salts, I took a short cut across the grass-plot, over which nothing but deities and senior fellows are allowed to walk. These things depressed my spirits; but I contrived to hold up by perpetually thinking on my father's dream, and the constellation of the Heavenly Ass, which supported me through all the gorgon terrors of deans, proctors, bishops, and senior fellows.

I did not indulge in many frolics at Cambridge, being naturally of a sober disposition; so that my juvenile wit never went beyond stealing a few rappers from the doors at night-time, and breaking half a dozen lamps between Cambridge and Barnwell; which, after all, I merely did to remove the odium of my being thought a quaker; and for which I was highly applauded by the young men of spirit and humour in this residence of learning. One more prank I must record, as leading to great consequences. Magdalene College is celebrated for its library, which a learned divine left to that establishment with the strictest clauses—no one can go into the library without three fellows at his heels—no book may ever be taken from the shelves; and if a volume is missing at the end of the year, the whole library is forfeited to another college; and if that college loses a volume, it forfeits the legacy to another college, and so on, all through the colleges; till having run through Cambridge, it is to go to Oxford; and, if Oxford should be careless, it is forfeited back to Cambridge. Such extreme caution is owing to the great value of the manuscripts, which hardly forty people have ever been able to see, owing to the suspicious jealousy with which they are guarded. Some friends of mine, anxious to cheat all the satellites that keep ward and watch over this precious library, proposed to me to break through the windows at night time, and having rummaged over all the treasures, to set off some fire works, in order to draw the college to this holy of holies, and shew how the sanctuary had been defiled. I agreed to the plan; for my curiosity was excited; and accordingly, at dead of night, we put a ladder against the window, removed the iron bars, and with a dark lantern entered this library of invaluable books. We broke open all the doors, ransacked the cabinets, piled the books and manuscripts in the middle of the floor, crowned the bust of Homer with a powdered periwig, and piled up a vast quantity of chairs and tables against the door, to be thrown down by the first comer. Having each stolen an old book, as an evidence of our exploit, we set off a roman candle and a rocket from all the windows at the same time; and then retreated through the window by which we entered, climbed the college walls, crossed the river, and set off to Ely, on horses that one of the conspirators had ready for us. The next morning we returned to Cambridge, and found all the town in an uproar. "Have you heard what has happened? have you been told who did it?" — "No; we know nothing about what you are talking of, we are just returned from Ely." — "Oh! the library of Magdalene College has been plundered! Such a loss! What will be done?" The bells were ringing to convene the senate; and the streets were blocked up by big-bellied doctors of divinity, red-nosed heads of houses, proctors, beadles, syndics, caputs, and all the faculties, hastening to the senate-house, to give council in so great

a calamity. Edicts were stuck up at every corner, with seals as big as a plate, signed by the
vice-chancellor, offering rewards to any one that
would turn king's evidence; and threatening all
the offenders with excommunication, expulsion, rustication, and humiliation. After a
week's tumult, and twenty-one sessions extraordinary, and thirty-five latin speeches, and one
hundred and eighty resolutions, printed at the
university press, and ninety proclamations—it
ended just where it begun—that they were to-
tally unable to know how to find out the
thieves, whilst we all the time were enjoying
the confusion.

When the danger was somewhat passed, we
met together in our rooms, to look at the books
which we had stolen. One was a small book of
three leaves, of a mahogany colour, bound in
scarlet Genoa velvet, embossed with gold, and
was— "*A Daintie and Cunninge Device to make
Peese Porrige with thryfte and economie;—
prynted by Master William Goslinge, near to
St. Margerite's Church, London, in the yeare
of Salvation 1469.*" The second treasure was a
manuscript letter of Henry the Eighth to the

Lord High Chancellor, in which he called him a *"stinking, nastie beastie, and foul divil; and that if he did not mend his mind, his bodye should be mended instead, bye shaving offe the head with a two-edged sword, so help him St. Bridgette."* But who shall describe the indescribable value of my spoil? It was a manuscript translation from a work of Cornelius Agrippa, *"De Bestiss:"*—part of which I will give.

"Beasts can speak, and he that doubteth the fact may read this booke. In the first month of the year, at the first moment of the full moon, having taken a mouthful of parsley, mint, and wormwood, stand on thy left foot and say these three words three times:

*   *   *

"Thou must then make a mess of two inches of a tallow candle, the hair of an ass's tail, the tooth of a horse that is broken-winded, a half-pound of witch-elm leaves, two she-snails, the parings of the toe-nails of a doctor of divinity, one drop of blood from a man learned in mathematics, three leaves of Aristotle's Eth-ics, and a pint of linseed oil. Of this pottage thou must eat sparingly forty days at sun-rise; thou must say three oaths a day, and never go to prayers; and if thou then gettest by heart the following litany, and sayest it in the ear of a donkey, on a sabbath-morn, at three in the morning, the donkey will answer thee; and thou wilt be able to understand from that moment all beasts clean and unclean, all four-footed and two-footed animals, and all that swim under the waters, and all birds, and reptiles that creep on their belly, and all insects of the earth."

———————

The litany, and all the sacred words, on which this science depends, I chuse to conceal; for I never intend that any one but myself should be able to hold converse with brutes, but am perfectly determined that the secret shall fol-low me to the grave. When I had read this manuscript, I quietly put it into my pocket, and told my friends that it was an old work of no importance, so very ancient that it could scarcely be decyphered. But when I went home, I immediately set about practicing the rules commanded by Cornelius Agrippa.

The only difficulty that I experienced in pursuing the secrets of the occult philosophy, was in making the sacred pottage, of which some of the ingredients were difficult to come at. The tooth of a broken-winded horse I got from one of Jordan's stable-boys, for sixpence; but the parings of the toe-nails of a doctor of divinity, and the blood of a man learned in mathematics, were not so easily purchased. After puzzling my brains to no purpose for a long time, I at last determined to commence a love-affair with the bed-maker of a very learned doctor of divinity of St. John's College, celebrated for his ecclesiastical and controversial writings; by which means I hoped to persuade her to bring me some of his parings as opportunity offered. The bed-maker was very coy, and skittish; but by dint of my romantic attachment, my beautiful sonnets, my pastoral ditties, and fervent, though delicate, approaches, I at length gained her affections, though it cost me one pound eighteen shillings in a new gown, and half a dozen of black worsted stockings; with two or three ribbons, to set off her old bonnet that the doctor had given her three years ago, in a mo-

ment of admiration. Her surprise was great
beyond description when I requested her to get
me some parings; but I told her it was only a
whim of mine, which I could not account for.
She said, she was sorry I had not spoken sooner,
for she had two days ago thrown into the fire
the very thing I wanted; and that, to her certain knowledge she should not be able to meet
with them for three months to come, as they
were the result of a ceremony that only took
place four times a year. At length the happy
day came! With what enthusiasm did I embrace
the little parcel! Tears of joy ran down my face;
and I pronounced the bed-maker the most
charming and invaluable of her sex. To gain
the blood of a man learned in mathematics, was
also very difficult; but my ingenuity supplied
the deficiency, and conquered all obstacles, so
great was the thirst after knowledge, and desire of fame! One of my guardians, a West Indian merchant, had sent me a turtle of the finest species; and by the help of this turtle I contrived to get what I wanted. I gave a large dinner party to the most learned and mathemati-
cal men of Cambridge, and took particular

pains to invite a great mathematician of St. John's College, whom I placed on my right hand side, and helped to the choicest morsels. This erudite gentleman is famed for his love of good eating; and to indulge him to the highest possible extent, I filled his plate five times with calipash, and four times with calapee; and made him drink two bottles of rhum punch before the cloth was removed. Of other things he eat in proportion; and after dinner dispatched two bottles of port, and two of claret. I concluded the evening with a large barrel of oysters, of which he devoured two-thirds; and a bowl of milk punch, of which he swallowed half; an amazing quantity of food for a single gentleman, in my opinion. After supper, he was seized with a surfeit and fainting fit; and I, watching the moment, immediately dispatched a messenger for a surgeon, who lived near at hand. The surgeon bled him copiously, by which the mathematician was relieved and I gained his blood, which I carefully bottled, and put by in a closet. Thus, by my perseverance, I gained what I wanted; and immediately proceeded to mix the pottage prescribed by Cornelius Agrippa; which

I solemnly protest, was one of the nastiest and most revolting things I ever tasted: not even excepting castor oil, which I used to consider the most disgusting thing in the universe.

CHAPTER II

Every morning, for forty days running, was I made to vomit by this nauseous magical potion; so terribly did it disagree with my stomach, nor was my joy ever greater than when the end of my troubles arrived. On the sabbath morn at three o'clock, I sallied out most punctually, and in Parker's Piece discovered a Donkey by moon-light, browsing on a thistle. With the greatest agitation imaginable, and my heart violently palpitating, I went up to the beast, and whispered in his ear the litany that I had carefully got by heart. Who can express my raptures, when the donkey answered me in intelligible words? I felt ready to faint for joy. — "Oh! Sir," said the ass, "how comes it that so great a magician as you deigns to speak to so miserable a wretch as me? For never since the days of Balaam and Cornelius Agrippa, has there been found a man on the earth able to confabulate with beasts.—Happy jack-ass am I, to have been the fortunate one to whom this wonder has been first revealed!" I embraced the donkey with enthusiasm, and shed tears of joy on his solemn face; and promised, that I would buy him of his present owner, at any rate. "I am glad, Sir," answered he, "to see that so great a magician has a tender heart; and trusting in the signs of benevolence that you shew, I will not hesitate to tell you that there is a grand conspiracy amongst all the beasts in the world, to liberate themselves from the tyranny of mankind; since there are few so generous and tender-hearted as yourself, or whose hands are not dyed in the blood of poor unoffending animals. I, for my part, Sir, was weaned at a very tender age from my mother, and loaded with heavy weights before my bones were thoroughly formed; so that you see all my legs look as if they had been broken; and having changed from one master to another, all thorough barbarians, was at last stolen by a gypsey, and he sold me to a chimney-sweeper, who now treats me with greater cruelty than any of my former masters. He never lets me walk an inch, without beating me with a great club that he keeps on purpose; and has taught his two sons to whip me with thorn-branches, and burn me with red hot irons; sometimes they all three together beat me with hedge-stakes, for mere amusement, solely because from extreme hunger and fatigue I cannot put one leg before another; and to such a pitch has their malignity proceeded, that I feel I am dying gradually of an ulcer of the spine, produced by incessant blows, kicks, and burns. This is a great affliction to me, as I fear that I shall not live to see the glorious emancipation of Brutes, and the humiliation of that tyrant, Man; which if I could but witness, I would gladly bear ten years more of suffering and misery."

We were here stopped short by the approach of the chimney-sweeper, who seemed much surprised to see me looking with such fixed attention on his donkey, at so early an hour; but I told him I had taken a fancy to the beast, and was anxious to purchase him. After much bargaining and higgling, I gave him twenty-six shillings, and rode off on the back of my friend and philosopher. We had not gone a hundred yards, before we were met by a herd of cattle, who, not imagining that I could understand them, began talking to my donkey. "Well, friend," said an old red cow, "are you going to work so soon? You have got a new master, it seems, who, I hope, will treat you a little better than the chimney-sweeper." "Oh, Mrs. Crumplety-Horn," answered the ass, "I have the honor to carry on my back a great magician who can understand every word we say, and who has bought me of my late master from mere compassion. I am sure he is meant by destiny to have a great part in the emancipation of Brutes; else how would such a magician come amongst us, on the very eve of the great rebellion? I propose that we introduce him to the chief conspirators in the fens of Cambridgeshire, and shew him every possible mark of esteem and veneration; for, doubtless, by his great power, he will be able to be of great service to the good cause." "I am happy," replied the cow, going down on one knee, "thus to shew my esteem for the great magician, for it is a rare thing to find a good man in all their race, to such a pitch of cruelty have they arrived. It was only last week, that one of them took away my poor little calf, scarcely nine days old, and sold it to a butcher, who yesterday morning passed down the lane with a cart-full of poor innocents, tied together in heaps, amongst which I noticed my little one; and when I ran bellowing after my poor darling, to be allowed at least to see it before they killed it, the infernal monster hit me a great blow on the head with a pitch-fork that nearly killed me. Reeling with pain, and bleeding as I was, I nevertheless followed at a distance, and saw them throw my young one into the slaughter-house like a lump of sand; and advancing still nearer, I saw them beat its brains out with a large sledge-hammer, amongst twenty other little creatures as young as himself, till the blood quite ran down the gutters in rivers. Some small revenge I had; for I waited till the butcher came out of the slaughter-house, when I rushed upon him, and gored him to death with my horns."

"And I," said a magnificent white bull, advancing up to me, with becoming reverence, "I must not omit to relate my wrongs to the great and benevolent magician; for yesterday I heard our tyrants agree that I should be publicly baited, in order to celebrate the election of a member who is supposed to be the advocate of liberty and humanity. At this baiting, I shall be tied by the nose to a stake, and torn to pieces by savage dogs; till, fatigued and overcome by extreme efforts to avoid my persecutors, I shall be tormented with burning faggots placed under my belly; wounds will be cut on my back, into which they will pour vitriol and turpentine, in order to excite me to farther rage, by the most dreadful bodily pangs that a poor animal can suffer; till at last, entirely unable to move a muscle, I shall be cut up by the butchers, and my flesh sold at a cheap rate to the wretches who have been enjoying my tortures." "Oh, my friends!" replied I, "spare me these dreadful accounts. Heaven knows I pity your misfortunes, and would gladly sacrifice my life to emancipate you from the dreadful tyranny under which you groan; but what can I do? And how can you be saved?" To this, the bull re-

plied, with a threatening aspect, "Great magician, our wrongs are beyond all endurance, and
every beast and animal in the creation is in a
league against Man, that monster and disgrace
of the works of God. We only wait for a proper
day, to rise universally, and destroy our oppressors; an attempt which may be expected every
day, and I assure you that very few will be
spared in the grand revolution that is medi-
tated." After a little further conversation, I
agreed to meet the conspirators in the fens of
Cambridgeshire, where all the plots and cabals
were agitated; and I returned home full of the
most afflicting thoughts, and unceasing wonder at all that had happened.

At night I could scarcely sleep for the tumult of my thoughts; and when I had, at last,
fallen into a doze, I was awakened by a small,
though shrill, voice in my ear, which thus addressed me. "Immortal wizard! I am a flea; and
in the name of all fleas, and as spokesman of
the bugs also, I come to declare that our tribes
have come to the unanimous resolution never
to bite you again, from the profound veneration we have for your superior knowledge, and

benevolent disposition; and in the approaching revolution, though our adversaries will not be allowed a moment's rest at night, yet you shall sleep sweetly, and without irritation; and we only pray you, as a return for our kindness, not to feel a loathing when you see us again in a bed; for we solemnly declare, we only infest your race to gain a livelihood, and should be the most miserable of insects, if so great a man felt any disgust on seeing us." "Illustrious fleas! philanthropic bugs!" answered I, "I gladly enter into this treaty with your race; for hitherto I have suffered much from your activity, and have received from you bites which give me pain to think of; nor can it be denied that I have sometimes cracked a flea, and squeezed a bug to death; but this was owing to temporary passion, and ancient prejudices which your magnanimous conduct has completely dissipated, and I solemnly declare that I will henceforward treat you with all the respect that you deserve." On this, the fleas and bugs retired in grand procession across my pillow, and deliberately marched out of the room, as an earnest of their good intentions, which gave me considerable satisfaction, as an armistice with gentlemen of so much consequence is of no small importance in my eyes.

After so agreeable a treaty, I slept without further disturbance, and rose early in the morning to go into the fens, about four miles from Cambridge, to meet the principal conspirators according to agreement. In passing along the streets, I was arrested by the lamentable tones I heard issue from the boards of a fishmonger's shop, and by the art I had acquired I could easily comprehend the conversation of the fish that were yet alive. A large regiment of crabs and lobsters were just put on the boards from a hamper that had been sent from Lynn; their claws were strongly tied up to prevent mischief, and they were yet black and lively. "Was there ever such cruelty heard of," said a large lobster to a she-crab; "here we are fished out of the sea by hundreds, and sent sixty miles in a hamper, to be boiled alive over a slow fire, in order to gratify the gross appetite of an old fellow of a college. Only see, I count thirty-four victims of yesterday's cooking, placed in a line before us, all dead, and of an unnatural colour, so that it is pretty certain we shall have the same fate in a very short time." "Alas! it is too true," answered the crab; "943 sons and daughters of mine have been boiled within these last three weeks; and last of all I have been caught also, though I kept at home as much as possible. My husband's entrails and legs were stewed in butter and pepper yesterday, and cooked up in his back, as a dish for an alderman of this town; and I have just been bought by a dropsical old lady, who declared that if I was put into cold water at first, and was boiled gradually on the fire, and served up with salad, I should be a capital morsel." "But what are your miseries to mine," said an oyster:— "for here are three hundred brothers and sisters of mine, all condemned to be torn asunder by great knives this evening, at a supper given by the master of St. John's College; and I verily believe that more of our race are destroyed at a single meal, than of any other unfortunate animal." "Courage, courage, fellow sufferers," exclaimed a silver eel, that the fishmonger had half-skinned, and was gradually depriving of its beautiful covering, by unrelentingly tugging with his bloody hands, in spite of the agony and writhings of his victim; "courage, my good friends: for great as is all our pain, and intolerable as is mine also, whose agony is more gradual and intense than any which you suffer, yet the day is near at hand, when every fish, and fowl, and beast will be emancipated; and when I hope a large proportion of the human race will be thrown to the sharks and swordfish, and when my elder brethren the conger eels will swallow the tyrants that have been so long tormenting us." The poor sufferer would have said more, but the fishmonger by a fresh tug entirely pulled off the skin, which threw the eel into such convulsions of pain, that after ten minutes spasmodic agony and violent contortions, it was relieved from its torture by a miserable death. "Water— water—water," cried out a dying trout, "water to save my life; for my tormentors have decreed that I shall be gradually drowned in air, and have already kept me ten minutes out of the bucket. Alas! what harm did I ever do in my native stream? Why was I separated from my speckled brethren, to be thus put to a slow death? My life has been spent in dancing up

and down the rivulet, without intending harm
to any one: but in an unlucky moment I have
been caught by the universal tyrant, whose hand
nothing can escape." Harrowed up with so
much complaining from sufferers that I could
not relieve, I hurried onwards, and in an hour
found myself at the place of rendezvous for the
conspirators. They were in the middle of a large
swampy common, which it was difficult to get
at: but when I was perceived at a distance, a
horse came galloping up to me, and when he
had approached within a few yards he drew
up, and falling on his knees, requested that I
would do him the honor to get on his back,
and ride to the meeting. Having made proper
acknowledgments to him for his civility, I got
on his back and was thus conveyed to the assembly, which consisted of cows, oxen bulls,
horses, dogs, sheep, and asses, who all made
me the most flattering reverence as I approached
them. The president of the meeting, who was a
bull, desired to know whether it was my pleasure to receive an address of congratulation by
a deputation of donkeys, that had been voted
to me, *nemine dissentiente*; and on my express-

ing myself too happy at the honor, four Jack-asses approached me, and the eldest, rearing up on his hind legs, thus addressed me:—

"In the year of Freedom, ONE."

"LIBERTY AND EQUALITY. The Brutes of Cambridgeshire and Ely, and Deputies from various places, being assembled in full conclave, beg leave to approach, with feelings of the profoundest respect and admiration, the immortal philosopher who has bro-ken through the secrets of nature, and the prejudices of his education, and has deigned to interest himself in the affairs of suffering creation. Great sir, we hail with joy your approach, and receive with rapturous enthusiasm your person, and your virtues, which words would in vain endeavour to express, and which flattery cannot possibly exaggerate; for when we con-sider the amazing profligacy and corruption of your species, and the dear love of tyranny and cruelty that animates every man living; and yet see you alone hu-mane, tender-hearted, and benevolent, we look upon you as a bright star in the heavens, that shines through the clouds of darkness and of tempest. Great sorcerer! The day is at hand when all the beasts, rising up in a body against their oppressors, will come in a victori-ous body to carol forth the hymn of happiness, at the shrine of reason and of liberty; and when, even amidst the praises of two such deities, your name will be chaunted in choral song, and with universal praise. Deign then, mighty magician, still to illuminate our minds, to assist at our counsels, and direct our plans. All that you dictate must be wisdom; all that you wish, must be virtue; and all that you execute, happiness and liberty for the sufferers that adore you."

————————

To this speech, which is so flattering that I hardly can bring myself to write it down, I answered shortly, and told them in a few words that I would do everything in my power to promote a cause which I so much admired; and my answer was received with a loud braying of asses, roaring of bulls, bleating of sheep, neighing of horses, and barking of dogs.

The business of the day was opened by admitting a deputy hackney-coach-horse from London, one of whose eyes was knocked out, who was spavined, and fired in all his legs, and had the grease in two of his heels. His ribs were unusually prominent, and there were two raw places on his shoulders and neck. "Brethren and fellow sufferers," he began, "I am deputed by the grand committee of the London United Brutes, to summon some of you forthwith to the capital to assist at the grand rebellion, which it is determined is to commence next Monday morning by sunrise; and I am ordered to give you the most consoling assurances of the likelihood of a great and speedy victory over our enemies and oppressors. Brethren, lovers of liberty, the sun of emancipation is rising in the political horizon; and the fogs of tyranny and prejudice are everywhere dissipated before that great and glorious luminary, whose fuel is virtue, reason, and equality. The emancipation of all beasts is written in the book by fate; and they who have so long governed us by bit and by bridle, by thong and by spur, will be driven from the dominion that ignorance first allowed, and cruelty afterwards cemented. The sufferings of our tribe alone are tremendous, and the thousands that are sacrificed to the pleasure and avarice of our tyrants every year is perfectly incredible. But I will not dwell on the recital of our wrongs, for we all suffer alike, and every species and genus of animals is equally tormented by the tyrant of the universe. Let us all then unite in perfect harmony; let all feuds be forgotten, and all ancient rivalries be eternally obliterated, that we may join in overthrowing that despotism which is the enemy of us all."

This high-minded speech of the deputy hackney-coach-horse seemed to electrify all present; and a most touching scene took place, of the reconciliation of animals formerly considered bitter enemies. The cow and the bull embraced the dog; the dog, the sheep and the cat; and the cat wept, in tears of fraternity and union, over the bosom of the rat and the mouse. The ferret shook hands with the rat, and the terrier kissed him also; till all present, in one unanimous sentiment, held up their tails to heaven, and exclaimed in the most determined tone, "We swear eternal friendship!" Never was I more touched; tears of sentimentality rolled down my cheek; and I felt for the first time the blessing of a virtuous friendship, in a cause which liberty has approved, and courage protected.

It was then agreed that a deputation of the conspirators should immediately set off to London; and that on the Monday next, at sunrise, all the animals in the county of Cambridgeshire should begin the rebellion, by resisting their masters in every point where obedience was required. The horses promised to kick the stable boys and farmers, and to overturn the stage coaches and stage waggons; the cows declared they would toss the milkmaids, and break down the enclosures; the dogs promised to bite every one they met; the cats to scratch, the rats to nibble, the donkeys to turn doubly obstinate, and the sheep, who had no powers of resistance, to run away from their masters, and seek their ancient liberty in uncultivated moors and desolate mountains.

With these resolutions the meeting broke up; and I promised the president to go with the deputation to London, and aid the conspirators with the best advice I was able to give.

CHAPTER III

I WAS BUT JUST in time when I arrived in London, for the very next morning the grand rebellion began, and I heard it everywhere said that the public conveyances were stopped, owing to the restiveness of the horses. The spirit of rebellion was evidently on the eve of a great eruption, which I could perceive as I walked along the streets; the horses of the hackney-coaches were all talking politics, with the greatest vigour, as they stood in their stations; and the most blind, lame, and miserable of them all, assumed a spirited and lively appearance, such as they never had shewn since they were weaned. Some of more enthusiastic dispositions could not wait for the general uproar, but indulged their patriotic spirits by rearing and kicking, and breaking the coaches to pieces. At night I went to the ground behind Russell Square, which is as yet appropriated to no purpose; where an ox that I met in Smithfield told me was to be the grand meeting of all the principal conspirators. The crowd was immense; and I heard the watchmen in grand consultation concerning this extraordinary assemblage, of cows and horses, that were pouring down the streets. Some thought it must be an overplus in the market, which the owners not having the power to sell, were driving home to the country. But then again, they were puzzled that no drover attended them, and the horses without any halter confused them beyond description. Though the meeting was so numerous, all was carried on with the greatest decorum, and modesty; and it was agreed that all animals should be invited to draw up a list of their grievances, and send them in by a deputy to the great committee, or grand council of secrecy; that the rebellion should commence on the morrow by sunrise; and that all who shewed any deficiency in courage should be considered enemies to the public cause;—that a remonstrance, dictated by the president, and written by my hand, should be presented to the king, or home secretary; and that if a favorable answer was not returned, no pause should be allowed in the warfare. A poodle-dog, a deputy from France, was introduced to the assembly; a merino sheep from Spain; a bouquetin from the Alps; a bear and a wolf from the Pyrenees; and various other animals from other countries, who gave the fraternal embrace, and were received with thunders of applause.

The address to the king, which the president composed, and I was requested to write down, was as follows:—

"To his Most Gracious Majesty, &c. &c.

"May it please you, sire, to receive this address of the birds, beasts, fishes, and insects of your united kingdom; who, with every feeling of respect for your august person, have nevertheless determined firmly and courageously to state their grievances, and call for reform.

Sire, nearly 6,000 years have passed away, without the slightest complaint from the animals subjected to man; and if there had been the slightest compassion shewn to us, in our state of servitude, we might yet have born our chains without complaint, and without resistance. But now, to such a pitch of abominable cruelty have our governors arrived, that it would be wickedness in us to bear the yoke any longer.

We beg leave to state to your august majesty, that at the table that is served up daily to your majesty, there are not less than twenty different animals sent up, after having been sacrificed by cruel and unrelenting tortures, merely to titillate your majesty's palate; and that two or three limbs of different animals are boiled down, merely to make sauce for some other limb, which cannot be produced from itself. We beg leave to state also, that at the suppers of your majesty's numerous household, there are frequently devoured live not less than a thousand oysters; and that whole regiments of small birds are roasted together at blazing fires, to feed your majesty's lords in waiting, and peeresses in their own right. Your majesty's beef-eaters are an abominable insult upon humanity, merely from their name; and it is incredible that a hundred such monsters should be clothed in scarlet and gold, and keep watch over your majesty's person with gold battle-axes, as if they were patronized by your majesty, and in high favor. These ruffians literally take their title from devouring whole herds of cattle, and are paid for that specific purpose. What would the world say, if your majesty were to keep a hundred man-eaters? And it ought to be remembered, that all cattle are the elder brothers of men, and were created before them. In your majesty's august and sacred stables, are several hundred horses, kept on delicious food, and pampered with every luxury, merely to corrupt their minds, and make them enemies to the liberties of their fellow sufferers; and this we consider a special grievance, and loudly calls for the dismission of these pensioners and place-holders of your majesty's household. The example that wicked men have persuaded your majesty to set to your subjects had had its due effect; and the lower orders of people have even outrun the cruelties practiced by your majesty's household. No one can be a moment now after sunset without torches made from the fat of murdered sheep, a burning shame of the nineteenth century; and all your lamps are kept blazing by the oil taken from whales, the monarchs of the fish tribe, who have been barbarously destroyed by hooked javelins, and barbed harpoons. Your majesty's soldiers can never go to war, without calling your sanguinary troops together by beating an instrument made out of the skin of that most harmless and unwarlike of animals, the sheep; so that, by a refinement in cruelty, those who are virtuous and innocent in their lives, are made cruel, wicked, and destructive, after their deaths! And, as if such barbarity were not sufficient, the same animal is made to serve purposes still more horrible and pestiferous; for not a single act of the lawyers can be valid these days, unless it is inscribed on the skins of mur-

dered sheep; and when one considers the horrible in-
iquity and cheating of the law, and the ruin and misery it causes to every one, it must be confessed that
this last contrivance is more cruel than the first.

"Sire, time would fail us to describe all our grievances; they are far too numerous to be related. Your
majesty's subjects scarcely ever open their mouths, except for our destruction; or close them, till they are
satisfied with our flesh. Our limbs and bones are scat-
tered in white and terrible heaps over all the land;
and the ground is enriched by our relicks, and fat-
tened by our deaths. The fields grow green in our destruction; and even nature smiles, when the carnage
of our race is more complete. The farthest lands under the sun are ransacked for some wretched animal,
whose blood is less common; and the deepest seas are
sounded, for some rare and unknown fish, to enrich
the tables of your priests and nobles. No clime is not
hunted for our death or our slavery; the bones of our
elephants serve as keys for your musical instruments;
the feathers of our fowls to write all that is bad, and
sign all that is noxious and deadly. Your feet are or-
namented by our scalps, and your backs kept warm
by our treasures. Your most dignified counselors sit
on a woolsack; and the most exalted prince is decorated in the skin of the ermine. All your looks,
thoughts, and wishes, portend ruin to the Brutes; and,
in cruelty so complete as this, all parties have united,

without the slightest remorse. Whig and tory, king and republican, aristocracies, oligarchies, and despotisms, are all alike our enemies; so that our afflicted and desolate tribes have no one to whom to turn the eye of supplication;—no one, from whom they can expect a moment's mercy, or a single word that promises compassion.

The hour is now come, sire, when a prophecy is accomplished, that all your divines and bishops have entirely neglected; though in a book which is read every day in the great churches. The words are these;-"he shall save both man and beast;" and our rebellion will bring these words to pass. Your august and sacred majesty ought not to forget that beasts were created before man: and that a thousand warriors have been destroyed by the jaw-bone of an animal which you chuse to denominate the most stupid and contemptible; that all countries have been originally possessed by us alone; and it is only by your encroachments and ambitious spirits, that you have gained possession of acres in which you have no legal share.

Sire, the earth is ours as well as yours. Freedom is the gift of God; and cruelty the invention of man alone;—and with such sentiments we have determined to regain our freedom, and break through the bonds which time seems almost to have hallowed. If, like a great and a good king, your majesty will rise up in the cause of the Brutes, we will still acknowledge your authority: but if you yield to the voices of pernicious counselors—then look to it; and remember four words that have made kings tremble long ago:—"*Mene, mene, tekel, upharsin!*"

Signed by the Directory,

HOUYHNHMN CHESNUT, Esq.
FAIRFIELD PARTRIDGE, Esq.
JOHN DOREE, Esq.
GREEN DRAGON-FLY, Esq.
CITIZEN SLUG.

LIBERTY!   EQUALITY!

————

This spirited and *manly* address, (if I may be allowed such an expression) was sealed by a curious seal; the device of which was a man and a monkey sitting on the same chair, and holding up a world between them; the monkey saying to the man, "*O formose puer minimum ne crede colori.*" On the reverse, King Nebuchadnezzar grazing amongst the cattle,—the legend;—"*Pro Rege, lege, Grege;*" of which the proper translation is, "*for the king, read, the flock.*"—This address I was ordered to take to —— immediately; to whose house I went accordingly without delay. It was one o'clock in the morning, and the house of the minister for the home department was filled with a large party called ministerial, by which is meant a collection of pensioners, whose loyalty and votes are kept in play by port wine and claret. The crowd was immense, and the carriages at my lord's door innumerable; but the horses, I observed, were all unruly, so elated were they with the prospect of their speedy emancipation. After having been shewn into six antechambers, and having marched through whole regiments of powdered lacqueys, I was introduced into the secretary's office—the gentleman who writes the minister's answers from the king to his people. "Sir," said I, bowing, "I have a paper of the greatest importance to deliver to the minister; who, I trust, will deliver it to the king before an hour is elapsed." "Of what nature is the paper?" inquired the under-secretary. "It is a petition of grievances, and a demand for reform, from—." "Oh!" said the undersecretary, "if that's the case, I will give you an answer immediately, without troubling my lord, or his majesty either; for I dismiss such matters as these very shortly." So saying, he briskly took

a fine sheet of fools-cap hot-pressed paper, perfumed with attar of roses, on which he wrote
the following answer:

> "Gentlemen,
>
> "I have presented to his majesty the address
> which you have done me the honor of forwarding to
> me, by Mr. Sprat; and beg leave to inform you that
> his majesty has commanded me to say, that he sees no
> grounds for attending to your petition.
>
> > "With sentiments of respect,
> >
> > "I remain,
> >
> > > "Gentlemen,
> > >
> > > "Your obedient, humble servant,
> > >
> > > > "_____."

"But, my dear Sir," exclaimed I, "do but read
the petition, before you give me such an answer;
the good of the whole nation depends upon the
king's taking the petition into farther consideration." "That's what reformers always say; and
I assure you I have general orders from the minister to put all reform petitions into the fire without looking at them, nor dare I disobey orders
so far as to except this from the general fate."
With this gracious answer, he handed the peti-

tion to a clerk, who handed it to a footman, who handed it into the fire; and I had nothing to do, but to pocket the affront, and his majesty's gracious answer, and walk out of the office. In going down the steps of the house, I was jostled by Lord Thunderbottom's servant, who was opening the carriage-door for his master, and the jolt I received pushed me against the Duchess of Straddle; her grace shrieked aloud, and instantly I was surrounded by a troop of lacqueys and young noblemen, who having given me a terrible caning, rolled me in the gutter, after a volley of execrations, which I bore quietly, as became a quaker and philosopher. This was the first time I had been introduced to the aristocracy of the land; that exalted privileged order, who, together with the crown, are ordained by providence to shower upon the land the blessings of subordination, and submission; and whose united weights so exactly balance the scale of government against the people, that a flea skipping on either scale would destroy the whole system of weights and measures, that all ages have agreed in praising as the most perfect of human inventions. Having risen out of the gutter, and shaken my ears as well as I was able, I marched off with the royal answer in my pocket, which I did not think would give much satisfaction to the rebels; and on my way to the place where the directory held its sittings, I amused myself with pleasing reflections on our excellent institutions, which allow of the wishes of the people to be thus easily disposed of by a clerk in office, without ever troubling the head of the nation whose head is filled with so much more serious matters. "The Routine of Office" was thus opened to my eyes; a mystery which all cannot comprehend; but which to me seems to consist in giving civil answers, and doing nothing. To me, however, it appears that the matter might be still more simplified; for if some ready printed answers were kept in the office of ministers, all signed and sealed for all occasions, there would be nothing wanted but a child to hand the answers out to the petitioners; and even that might be done by a small patent steam-engine, made express for the purpose, in the most economical manner possible.

As I have now brought this history to a most interesting point, when the grand rebellion was

on the eve of a general eruption, I must just stop
the course of the narrative a little, to let my readers know in what manner I was a sufferer and
martyr in the cause of liberty; for it would be
impertinent in me to do so, when the great war
had once began. It may be remembered that one
of the articles of the potion prescribed by
Cornelius Agrippa, was the parings of the toe-
nails of a doctor of divinity, which I only could
procure by a stratagem, and by commencing an
amour with a bed-maker of St. John's College.
As soon as I had gained what I wanted, I deserted the lady to whom I was so much indebted,
a piece of ingratitude and perfidy which will
wound my heart to the last moment of my life;
which even now makes me shed tears, and gives
me a great pain in the stomach, whenever I think
of it. And the only consolation I have, in reflecting on this black spot in my morals, is that Ja-
son treated Mrs. Medea in a manner precisely
similar; and that several great men besides have
been *quite as base* as I have, not forgetting Æneas
and a more modern example. It is one part of
repentance to have courage to confess sins; and
as I have done so, it somewhat relieves my con-

science, and will, I hope, be a warning to any single gentlemen that read this shocking part of my history, that may have behaved in a similar manner, to make up for their perfidy as well as they can, by any honorable and gentlemanly method. The bed-maker, whose name from delicacy I will repress, finding that I had deserted her as soon as she had given me the doctor's toe-nails, fell into several swoons and fainting-fits; and cried till her beautiful nose and eyes were quite red with weeping; and finding that I answered none of her letters, and paid no attention to her complaints, she fell ill of the cholic, and grew so lamentably thin, that her ribs might all have been counted; so much were her feelings wounded by a sense of slighted love. After some days of useless complaints, revenge supplanted love; and desperate with her passions, in a moment of rage, she went to the doctor, and told all my plans to procure his toe-nails. Now, by the statutes of Cambridge, the little finger of a doctor of divinity, or other dignitary, is declared to be of greater value than the lives of ninety and nine students in *statu pupillari*, provided they be not noble; and from this *lex consultissima,* it follows as an immediate deduction, that an under-graduate who steals anything from people so immensely his betters, is guilty of as great a crime as the theft of Prometheus, that abominable and deadly sin, which brought women and wickedness into the world. The doctor was in a rage beyond all description; he rent his black academical, double-Lyons, silk-Sunday gown; he threw his perriwig into the fire, and turned over two chairs and a table; and kept demanding of the bed-maker why I had robbed him, and what use I could make of his excrescences? This the lady could not explain; but she suggested all sorts of horrible causes, and goaded him with hints the most cruel and agonizing. Thus a gentle heifer irritates a lordly bull, which some gad-fly is biting; and by her presence, and her balmy breath, stirs him up to encreasing madness. The doctor instantly convened me to appear before the seniority; but I, having left Cambridge, did not receive the summons, and consequently did not attend it; and was thus condemned of two crimes — *"lese majesty and contumacy;"* and was expelled from that learned and enlightened university, from which I had

taken so much without giving any thing back.
The proctor in the civil courts, who pleaded my
cause before the vice-chancellor in my absence,
endeavoured to prove that I was *noble* by birth;
a hard task for any but a lawyer, in any place
but Cambridge; for if you get at a king in the
herald's office, a hundred generations ago, in
your family, you are by academical law considered noble, and may get all the blessings that
always attend nobility. The learned proctor undertook to prove that I was descended from
Bruce, king of Scotland; which he said was *prima
facie* evident from the name; for what etymolo-
gist did not see the identity of Bruce and Sprat?
"Bruce, Bruty, Brut, Brat, Sprat;" and he produced an ancient dusty manuscript (made the
preceding evening in his chambers) to prove that
a great, great aunt, great seventy-nine times back-
wards, bore a child to the twenty-ninth nephew
of King Bruce; and as the birth took place in
Scotland, such a birth constituted a good marriage; and that consequently I was of blood royal,
and ought to take an honorary degree. An ex-
ception was taken to this, by the proctor employed by the doctor; and replications and pa-

pers were written, enough for all the water-clos-
ets in Cambridgeshire; but the vice-chancellor
got over my nobility; and I was expelled in spite
of my civilian, who appealed to the king in chan-
cery; and the chancellor having given my case a
hearing about four years ago, has promised to
hear it again in ten years time; when, I hope justice will be done to me, my nobility proved and
I recover my state in Cambridge, besides gaining a nobleman's degree. The fair bed-maker
having procured my expulsion, and thus satisfied her revenge, felt a return of pity and of love,
which, I am told, is the usual phenomenon in
such cases; and she took it terribly to heart that
she had injured one whom she loved so much.
The matter preying upon her mind more and
more, and finding that the doctors could do her
no good, and that castor oil and poultices made
her rather worse than better; and that by her
revenge she had cut off all hopes of reconciliation;—she determined to quit this scene of tribu-
lation and vanity, by putting an end to herself
without waiting for death to come of his own
accord, and hand her to her coffin. With such a
determination, she collected all the gifts I had

presented to her, in the days of our tenderness; a large flowered printed cotton gown; half a dozen of black-worsted stockings; a pair of shoes and pattens; a pair of red garters; my old broad-brim hat, which I was ashamed of wearing at Cambridge; three love letters, and five love songs; together with all her wardrobe, which she piled together in the middle of her bed-room, and set on fire. Having stuck herself with a carving knife, she jumped her last jump on the funeral pile, and was found afterwards a half consumed skeleton on the floor. The flames set the house on fire, and that house set others on fire; and thus ten houses were consumed in succession, which proved what an inflammable thing love is, and how bad a man I am, though a quaker and a magician. My reflections here become so very painful, and I feel such twitches and spasms about the pericordium, that I am obliged to finish the chapter, hoping that my failings will be a useful example to other gentlemen, that may honor my narrative with a reading.

CHAPTER IV

WAR, HORRID WAR, and Thames all foaming blood, I see:—for, as soon as Aurora began to sow the earth with orient pearl, the grand rebellion of the beasts began, throughout all the world. O citizens! why did you wage these wars more than civil? Why did jack-ass fight with jack-ass; and men with monkeys, where there was such a fraternal similarity between you? Why did discord divide such real brothers? particularly when Englishmen might have been better employed in fleecing the French of the monuments of art that they yet possess; and when her heroes of Waterloo are wandering about, in unrevenged shades? How much land you might have acquired by all this blood-shed! how many republics and free governments,

Lord Londonderry and Prince Metternich might have suppressed! The Spaniards might have been made to pass under the yoke; and the Neapolitans, and Greeks, perfectly annihilated, but for this war of brothers! The allied armies might have restored the ancient *regime* in France; and old Louis and feather-beds suppress the fire of insubordination that is manifest in the kingdom of lilies.

At six o'clock in the morning, the din was universal in the streets of London. All the hackney coaches were broken to pieces in the streets; and thousands of people kicked to death by revolutionary jack-asses, and republican geldings. The people had not slept a wink all night, owing to the vigorous attacks of the fleas, bugs, and gnats; the king had scratched himself till the blood came; and all the peeresses in their own right had kicked and tumbled about so, on their soft feather-beds, that they were thrown into a perfect fever. The ghosts of the geese on whose down they were lolling, flapped round their beds at midnight, let loose from Tartarus by Pluto, and nibbled their noses, and cackled dismal tones of horror and revenge. Frogs and toads came crawling into every moveable, and every utensil of every manner. ——house was full of frogs; his majesty found a Surinam toad bobbing about in his cup of chocolate; and a great bull-frog began croaking in the royal tea-pot: slugs and snails crept into the pockets of the lords in waiting; the beef-eaters were stuck in the guts by rampant oxen; and the poet-laureat was nibbled by an owl, and kicked by a donkey. All the court was in dismay; his majesty set off full gallop to ——, but the horses having taken him a little way overturned the carriage, and left their gracious sovereign in the mud! The house of commons received a sudden call; but a great beetle flew into the speaker's mouth, when he began to open the business of the day. The right hon. foreign secretary was stung by a hornet behind; and a couple of earwigs crept into the ear of the chancellor of the exchequer. In the upper house, the lords on the woolsack were overturned by two furious rams that came rushing into the chamber of peers; the lord chancellor could not speak, for he had swallowed a frog which stuck in his throat; a baboon took possession of the throne: and a great flock of geese began a grand chorus of cackling that entirely put an end to all business. A resolution having been passed that the kingdom was in danger, and that the privy council should see that the kingdom suffered no detriment, the house was hastily broken up, and the lords and commons got off as well as they could.

Though the rulers suffered so much, the people suffered equally; for all the streets were strewed with bodies of dead people; and mad dogs, mad bulls, and slimy frogs, were running riot in all houses. The plagues of Egypt never could have been greater; no one could leave his door, but a troop of wild furious horses was at his heels; and if he escaped into some corner where horses could not follow, a savage dog, or a venomous reptile was sure to be in at the death which others had commenced. All the china, glass, and jewel shops were broken to pieces by mad bulls; and a cloud of hornets and wasps penetrated into every recess, and searched every corner. It was a fearful sight to behold so many wretches scampering down the streets, closely pursued by wild horses and furious cattle, without the slightest hope of escape, or release from their misery; realizing all that one sees in a horrible dream, when the mind is oppressed with grief, or the body tortured by disease. The screams of terrified women resounded in every avenue; men and children were equally helpless, and all was one scene of terror, confusion, uproar and destruction. At night the order of things was reversed; and a committee of donkeys and monkeys met in the seat of legislature. The business was opened by repeated acclamations, and several resolutions were passed to establish on a firm basis the liberty of brutes. At length, the "Rights of Brutes" were voted by unanimity, as a standard of all future action, and the basis of every future relation between man and beast.

RIGHTS OF BRUTES.

I.

Nature has made brutes and men equal, the distinctions necessary for social order are only founded on general utility.

II.

Man is a two-legged, unfledged animal, without talons, or tail.

III.

No brute can be submitted to the power of man, without his consent.

IV.

Without the assistance of animals, man would have remained on a perfect equality with the beasts of the forest.

V.

The reason of man principally consists in his fingers, which are ten in number; for if the wrist of man had been terminated by a hoof, instead of a hand, no art or science could have been discovered, nor any knowledge gained.

VI.

Brutes are, generally speaking, stronger than men.

VII.

No man could live a month without the assistance of brutes:—at least the customs of society have made this intrinsically true.

LIBERTY!—FRATERNITY!—EQUALITY!

————

The debate then turned upon the mode of carrying on the rebellion, so that it might end in something of real interest to the parties that had undertaken it; and now for the first time, were found dissentions in the councils. The parties were three;—the Ultra-Liberators, that secretly wished for the total destruction of the race of man; the Liberators, who wished a separate interest to be formed between man and brute, by which one should mutually assist the other; and the Enemies of the Rebellion, or Anti-Liberals, who were secretly playing the part of the tyrants; and these were the king's horses, who having been long used to warm stables, and plenty of corn, were mortal enemies to the new order of things that deprived them of all their luxuries. These parties contended grievously amongst one another; but it was evident that the ultra-revolutionists were gaining ground; and could swallow up every thing by their violence and fury; and their party was much strengthened by several foreign brutes that had come over; amongst these were tigers, baboons, and wolves. These creatures brought over letters from the revolutionists on the continent, one of which I will copy.

"LIBERTY AND EQUALITY! HUZZA!!!"

"The Alpine Directory of emancipated Brutes, con-

sisting of Citizen Grim-chops, Citizen Munch-
bones, Citizen Lank-jaws, Citizen Big-tooth, Citizen Lean-belly, Citizen Lap-blood, send the fraternal embrace to the Brutes of England.

"Dear brothers and brutes,

"The torch of liberty, lighted at the altar of nature,
by the hands of reason, irradiates the universe with its
dazzling beams; and the shackles of servitude are broken, to the tune of the music of the spheres.—The hearts
of tyrants faint within them; and the clouds that obfus-
cated the disk of the great luminary, EMANCIPATION, are
dissipated in the shape of malignant mists which never
more shall dim the horizon, or cloud the atmosphere.
Brutes! It is decreed that our tyrants shall fall. Brutes! It
is decreed that we should regain our station in creation,
and not be finally obliterated from the book of nature.
Assume then an imposing attitude! Blow the trumpet of
liberty! Raise the standard of independence! Remember
that you are Brutes! and shew yourselves worthy of that
venerable name.

"By letter, we cannot send you more than the most
ardent expressions of encouragement and attachment;
but we burn to give you the fraternal embrace;—we
languish to bestow the lick of philanthropy.

"Dear brothers, send a deputation of your most
trusty heroes, with whom there may be an unre-
strained interchange of fraternity and love;—let us

draw nearer in bonds of union;—let us tighten the cords of love, and the links of philanthropy! Send us a deputation of your finest young lambs. We have always admired their unsophisticated patriotism, and we long to embrace the south-down heroes, of whose good qualities the world says so much. It is time that all the beasts of the world should be closely united; and that our tyrants, having the evidence of our unanimity, should rush in despair into the dens of darkness, and hide their heads in terror and cowardice.

"You will be rejoiced to hear that we have upset the government of Berne. We came in a body from the mountains, ate up the syndics in the market-place, liberated the town bears, and declared the first era of Liberty and Equality, after a grand procession in the central square of the city.

"Long live Liberty, Equality, and Independence!"

————————

I can by no means give an accurate account of the war, as I was not sufficiently in the secrets of the parties, to know much that was going on, beyond what every one has heard; but if any thing occurs to me, not yet published in the papers, I will faithfully notice it.

I remember, a little after this time, that some old broken-down horses at Dover, that had been condemned to feed the kennels, but had escaped from their owner, intercepted a king's messenger who was traveling with dispatches from the court of Vienna to London; and, by aid of the horses that were drawing his carriage, but who were well-affected to the cause of liberty, they contrived to upset him, and rob him of his portmanteau. Several letters were found in it of considerable importance; but one I particularly noticed, (for I was kindly allowed to copy it by the insurrectionary brutes) and it run thus:—

"To ——, London.

"The Emperor, my master, has heard with concern and alarm, of the rebellion of the Brutes that has broken out in England; and he has desired me to say, that he considers it the ramification of a great plot that has been hatched throughout all Europe, by the seditious and ill-affected members of society; who, being enemies to social order, are desirous to plunge Europe into the horrors of war, anarchy, and revolution.

"The liberals, free-masons, patriots, and other incendiaries, whose odious machinations the high and puissant members of the most holy alliance have so anxiously endeavoured to suppress, stung to madness with a sense of the loss they have sustained, and despairing of other means of liberation, have, it seems, at last leagued with the brutes of creation, and joined common cause against the monarchs, and the social order of Europe; hoping, by this unnatural league, to restore the reign of chaos and darkness.

"The Emperor, my master, earnestly begs that you will convince the members of his Britannic majesty's government, how necessary it is, in the present crisis, to strain every nerve to crush the first efforts of the incendiaries; and wishes me to state, that the means he has adopted in this new rebellion, are to suppress all the universities of Germany; to throw all free-masons into dungeons; to prohibit all newspapers; to create a strict censorship on the press; and to allow no books to be printed, but such as relate to botany, concology, dancing, and other general subjects; to put all suspected persons under arrest; to call in all editions of the Bible; to send for several opera dancers to amuse the people; and finally, to execute twelve donkeys in the great square of Vienna, as a terror to all rebellious beasts—these donkeys having been conspicuous for their liberal notions, and their attachment to free-masonry. If these, or any other measures of a stronger nature, should appear to you adviseable in this most alarming crisis, the Emperor, my master, hopes that you will zealously urge them on the consideration of the other members of government; and he desires me to assure you, that when these, or stronger measures, shall have been adopted in your country, there will be ready for your acceptance £100,000 sterling, as an earnest of the great consideration his imperial majesty has for your splendid talents, and your attachment to social order.

"By dispatches received this day at Vienna, from St. Petersburgh, his imperial majesty is assured, that his imperial majesty the Autocrat of all the Russias is ready to send into England seventeen hundred thousand calmucks, provided that their horses will keep quiet, and that the English parliament will pay for the expense of the expedition; which, doubtless, may be managed by judicious concessions to the country gentlemen, by increasing the severity of the game laws, and adding to the revenues of the church:— all which suggestions it is doubtless unnecessary to name, to a person of your excellency's approved foresight, and profound diplomatic talents."

"(Signed,) M —— ——."

————

The parliament were not slow in adopting strong measures for the suppression of the bestial rebellion; they voted a property tax of eighty per cent, and a loan of a hundred millions, with two millions to be raised by lotteries; they formed a committee to look into a green bag two yards deep, filled brim-full with lies; another committee, to enquire into the best means of removing the few remaining liberties of the people, and to make a report thereon; another committee of grievances and apprehensions; another of fears and doubts; another of strong measures; and when the minister got up in the house, and assured the members that the time was come for finally burning and destroying the Magna Carta, all the country gentlemen rose in their seats, and with three loud huzzas the bill for burning the Magna Carta was read the first time, and the cheering of the minister lasted for an hour and a half!

The beasts, however, did not remain idle, and such an army was approaching on the capital, from the north, of brutes, birds, and insects, as was enough to make the stoutest hearts tremble. They were instigated too by the most burning thirst of revenge, and the most alarming instigations of fear; for if the Emperor of Russia could but land his calmucks, they dreaded that their old masters would be too strong for them; and then such a slaughtering would there be amongst them as would well nigh tend to their total extinction! The Duke

of ——was appointed generalissimo of all the
forces sent by parliament to attack the brutes,
and the great hero of ——burned to finish the
column of his victories by this last most glorious triumph. War however at last declared
against him; and in a pitched battle fought on
Hounslow Heath, he, and all his forces were
routed, and the duke himself compelled to deliver up his sword to a fat Lincolnshire goose,
which had thus the honour of disarming the
great captain! All the world knows what followed—how the old triad of king, lords, and
commons was abolished—how the church was
destroyed—how the country gentlemen were
ruined—and all ranks of society shaved smooth
down by the razor of liberty.

CHAPTER V

I HAD SAID BEFORE that dissention and intrigues had risen in the army of the brutes,
which was much fomented by the king's horses;
and now that the fear of the enemy was at an
end, and there was more leisure for plots and
manœvering, such schisms and quarrels daily
arose amongst the liberators, that the new republic seemed threatened with speedy dissolution. The meetings of the beastly republic were
held on Salisbury Plain. A bull was the president, because he could roar loudest: and indeed his voice was much wanted in a senate
that consisted of twenty thousand individuals
at least. When a division took place, such a
galloping and dust there was, that a whole army
of Turkish cavalry was nothing to it. The par-

ties consisted of the royalists, or horses called in derision the "*Chalinophilists*" or "*lovers of bits,*" who had always wished for a moderate monarchy:—the rats who were ultra-royalists, and liked all old rotten rubbish:—the tigers, panthers, and hyenas, that were for military despotism:—the horned cattle, that were moderate constitutionalists:—the sheep, goats, and deer, which from their gregarious nature were republicans:—the ravens and kites, high democrats:—and the hawks and vultures, furious terrorists. The most ambitious and designing of all the animals was the ass, who evidently was making his party stronger and stronger every day. It was astonishing to see with what dexterity he managed to gain ground on all opponents; and still more astonishing to find that such a dumb patient creature, as he had hitherto been considered, should, now that matters were changed, shew such ambition and power of intrigue. But I explained it by the well known fact that those who have been long in a state of servility, are most likely to be corrupt in principle, and fond of dominion, and when by accident they have got power, to abuse it most odiously. Sure it was, that the ass stuck at no principle of honor, or qualms of conscience in strengthening his party; and it was all along clear to me, that he would be the Mark Antony of the brutes, unless he was taken off by some more powerful party. The convention of animals had never yet agreed upon a constitution, but seemed content to be directed by circumstances: every one seemingly acquiescing in the opinion that it was expedient to form a pure democracy, and every one trusting to some one else to effect it. The horse faction were the first that openly spoke against the republic; and they were such an impetuous, honest race, that they did not care what they said. The head of the horse faction was a cream-coloured stallion of the king's stables; a most noble beast, sprung in a right line from some famed Arabian favourite, and having in his veins the noblest blood of the best racers in the kingdom: his name was Buchephalus; and he was completely governed by his wife, a most beautiful full-blood black mare, of whom he was dotingly fond, and by whom he had several colts and fillies. She however was more beautiful than good, for it was strongly suspected that she intrigued with the ass, for reasons best known to herself; though it did appear odd that she should prefer such a mean animal, to so noble a beast as her husband. Scandal however was very strong against her, though Buchephalus never heard a word of it, nor could he have believed it; so thoroughly did he despise his ugly rival, and so completely did he hate and detest his servility and cunning.

Buchephalus having a high notion of his blood one day made a speech in favour of nobility and titles; and strongly urged that an aristocracy should be formed as a matter of justice and policy to all parties, and as holding out rewards to those that served the state. On this the sheep, the republicans, the terrorists, and all the popular party, made a great outcry; and the ass, seeing how matters stood, mounted the tribune, and in a speech full of dry wit ridiculed and exposed the vanity of the horse so completely that Buchephalus had not a word to say for himself in reply. He proved from scripture, that asses were of old the royal animal for kings in the East; and that if the foolish notion of titles was to be admitted, that they had much better give dignity to the ass than the horse, as it was quite a modern notion to think the horse a finer animal. Then he shewed that their late oppressors had always made horses dog-flesh when they died; and that nine out of ten were marred in their sex, in order to keep up anything like a decent breed; and that after all, not one in a hundred was worth looking at, as a fine animal. He next asked the horse, if his cropped tail was to be a sign of his nobility? (for Buchephalus had not much tail,) or whether he would wear a bridle as a mark of distinction? or shew his broken knees to prove his rank? At all this, the republicans were highly delighted, and made a most tremendous noise in approbation, applauding the donkey for this speech, and crying out that he was "The friend of the people—the father of his country!" The fox, who was ready to side with any party, and take advantages from all, next attacked him; then a magpie chattered a whole hour on the blessings of equality; then a parrot took up the cudgels; till at last the horse was in such a rage that he left the convention at a full gallop, and all his party after him. Now all that remained, who hated the horses for their family pride, vied with one another in thanking the donkey for the service he had rendered them, and it was voted unanimously "That what the horse had said was dangerous to the state; and that articles of impeachment should be made out against him, the execution of which was to be entrusted to the ass, and a committee of eleven other beasts."

The horse went in a furious rage to his wife, and told her all that had happened in the senate; and how the ass had turned him into ridicule, and put him to shame in full convention; but he said he would immediately send a challenge to him, and would soon shew how mean and despicable a creature he was, when it came to real courage and blood. The mare his wife, whose name was Camilla, had some difficulty in dissuading him from his purpose; but at last her love and blandishments prevailed, and he unwillingly consented to defer the challenge till the morning, when she knew she could find some other means to prevent his bloody intentions. At night-fall she sallied out to meet her lover, the ass, whom she speedily consoled for the fears he entertained of the rage of Buchephalus; and it was there agreed between them, that her husband should next day go to the senate; should adhere to what he had said; or even make more insolent proposals; and that he should then be arrested as a traitor to the republic, and given up to the power of the convention. All this succeeded to admiration: poor Buchephalus was arrested, and was tried with great solemnity for his crime against the republic: and was finally condemned to lose his sex, and be reduced to that state which so many horses in the world have to deplore. His wife soon after this got a writ of divorce against him, and publicly married the ass, by whom, two months after marriage, she had a fine mule, which was considered by the philosophers a perfect phenomenon, when it was remembered how short a time they had been married.

The horse faction grew desperate on the mutilation of Buchephalus, and immediately declared open war against the republic. The convention named the ass generalissimo of all their forces; who, with the help of the tigers and hyenas, completely routed the rebels, and returned in triumph covered with glory and laurels. He was received by the convention of brutes in a dress of state. The bull made him a speech of compliments, and presented him with a thistle, which was ordered to be the national emblem of glory; and it was carried by acclamation, that a pillar was to be raised to his genius, in which he was to be styled, "Parens, Bestiarum, Belluarum, Ferarum, Reptilium, Piscium, Insectarum, Avium Asinus, semper invictus, pius, amans patriæ, victor, clemens, triumphalor splendissimus": — The ass received all this with the utmost modesty: — he disclaimed all merit; he said that if success had crowned his humble efforts, it was all the favor of the invisible genius of the confederation of the brutes, which supported the cause of liberty by its divine protection: that, for his part, all that he wished as his reward, was to know that he had done his duty; that Liberty and Equality were the sole object of all his efforts; and that if the confederacy of animals chuse to condemn him to the meanest office, he would as gladly receive it, as their present most unexpected, and most undeserved honors; for all that the republic willed, was perfectly wise and good.—Indeed, so very little did he feel himself fit for the overwhelming load of renown that he had now to bear, that for his part, he had much rather go and live in retirement and honesty, on some unknown, unfrequented common, where the reflection that he had done his duty would be to him the dearest, brightest, sweetest reward, that brutes could devise, or gratitude invent. All this he finished with a flood of tears, and pathetically asked the bull's leave to go to his beloved retirement, which he solemnly swore was the wish nearest his heart. On this, the bull set up a great roar; he declared that the state would suffer an irreparable loss, if he left them, and that he never would consent to put the question. Here the whole assembly set up a loud shout, and surrounded the ass with tears, begging and praying him to live for the republic and not retire from the world. The fox, seeing how matters were tending, and having lately been bribed by a fat goose from the ass, mounted the tribunal, and, at last gaining silence, proposed to elect the ass as consul of the state. This was received with loud applause; but a spaniel, determined not to be outdone, rose and moved as an amendment that he should be styled *Perpetual Dictator;* and though the republicans loudly exclaimed against this, it was carried by uproar and confusion, though no division took place, that the ass should be *Perpetual Dictator;* and he was led by his faction to the chair, which he took with dignity and composure. There, turning up his eyes to heaven, and kneeling meekly on the turf, he thus took the oath of office: —

"I swear by the gloriousness of creation, by yon bright orb of light, by the genius of Liberty, more bright than the sun, and by the cause of Equality, sacred throughout the universe, that I will without fraud or dishonesty, execute my holy office, to the best of my abilities, for the sole good and benefit of beasts, birds, insects, reptiles, and fishes. — I will uphold the cause of liberty and equality; and all that are against it shall be my enemies; and I will live and die for my country."

This patriotic oath was heard with enthusiasm not to be described, by all the ass faction, which was now very strong; and though the republican sheep were sulky on the occasion, yet were they completely overpowered by the majority of the assembly; and when the meeting broke up, a procession was formed to the altar of the republic, where by the hands of the owl, (considered the high-priest of the animals) a hecatomb of a hundred parsons was offered up to the genius of liberty, who were now very naturally treated as the beasts of creation; for so completely were things changed, that to bear the shape of a man was held the greatest of disgraces; and the few human beings that remained, were kicked at and abused, if ever they presumed to make their appearance before their lords and betters, the brutes.

The ass, who was daily clearing the way to the throne, fomented a sedition amongst the animals, that he might reap the advantage from it. He secretly intrigued with the rats, or the ultra-royalists, and persuaded them to set up the claims of the lion to monarchy, he having been once the old king of the beasts; and then by threatening to side with them, he so frightened the republicans, that in order to avoid the old despotism of the lion, they immediately came over to his party; so that the ass and the sheep were now united against the lion, who was finally put to death with all his friends, the rats.

The next step was to take the lovers of military despotism, and the terrorists into favor; who, by their savage cruelties upon friends and foes, so alarmed the sheep, deer, goats, and horned cattle, that all the moderate republicans and constitutionalists were driven into a civil war; and, in order to save the constitution, to oppose with all their might the alarming power of the dictator donkey. The terrorists and high democrats had now no way to turn, to save themselves and their party from the constitutionalists, but by putting all into the hands of the ass; who sallied out against the sheep faction with a well appointed army, and utterly routed his opponents in a pitched battle, in which the constitutionalists did prodigies of valour to no purpose, for fortune was still with the dictator, who being himself a personal coward, had nevertheless selected such experienced officers, that his enemies fled before him like chaff in the wind. Our dictator returned with fresh glory to the convention of animals, who met him with still louder acclamations than

ever, and now begged him to finish the renown
of his virtuous life, by accepting a pension from
the state of a hundred thousand thistles per annum, and a large common to browse in,
"where" they added, *"you may repose for the
rest of your life, the Hercules of Animals."*

The dictator swore that that was the wish of
his heart; and retired home to tell the disagreeable news to his wife Camilla, that in reward of
his services the ungrateful creatures now wished
him to retire from public life; which if he consented to, would ruin all his plans for ever.
Camilla told him that nothing was now left for
him, but to dissolve the convention; for if he
refused to do so, they would certainly put him
to death; and that to save himself he must dissolve the meeting next day, and declare himself
absolute monarch. In vain did Camilla endeavour to instill courage into him, sufficient for so
daring an undertaking; and finding, after a night
of arguing, she could make no impression on
him, she undertook the task herself; and, with a
remnant of the dictator's victorious army, violently entered the assembly of beasts, who looked
at one another in mute astonishment and de-

spair. Having kicked the president from his seat, she thus spoke her mind:

"BEASTS!

"My husband, the Dictator, had done more for you than you can ever repay: and yet, notwithstanding his splendid services, you have thought to bribe him off, and make him leave the state open to your profligate and unprincipled intrigues. But you are mistaken. My husband is so hurt at your ingratitude, that he does not deign to see you again. I, therefore, being his natural representative, do hereby dissolve the confederation of animals, and declare all its acts null and void. The confederation has been a means of infinite wickedness and bloodshed:—it is time to dissolve it:—justice and reason call aloud for this act; for never were so many scoundrels and villains met together for the pretence of legislation. Go to your homes, wicked wretches! And ponder on the infinite mercy of the Dictator, who kindly allows you to live!"

Great was the hubbub, and sore the dismay at this unheard of violence; some called aloud for justice; others called Camilla an adulteress; and some proposed to resist force by force. Camilla however speedily put an end to this uproar, and her beasts of war, without much difficulty, dispersed the senators, who scampered home in dismay, and never again met to deliberate on affairs of state.

The infinite mercy, however, of the dictator did not rest here; and the next morning there were found dead one hundred and thirteen sheep; seventy-five oxen; two hundred stags; and fifty ravens; and after this the whole race of animals, birds, and beasts, and fishes, kept in their respective elements, as quiet as possible, for fear of offending the tyrant Ass.

CHAPTER VI

SHORTLY AFTER THE dissolution of the wittenagemot, or mickle-synoth of animals, a decree was issued by the Ass, of this nature:

"JOHN, by right hereditary, Ass and King, known of old by the name of Jack-Ass, of the illustrious house of Donkeys, to all Brutes, Beasts, Quadrupeds, Bipeds, Polypusses, flying and swimming Birds, Fish, Shell-fish, amphibious Animals, and Reptiles, health and asinine benediction.

"KNOW YE, that whereas of old, before the creation of man, animals (so called) had possession of the earth; and did enjoy rights, natural, civil, and religious; and were lords and masters of the world; and did flourish in great concord, peace, and harmony, under the guidance of our dear progenitors, Asses and Mules, illustrious princes, now with the MAMMOTH:—which said dear progenitors were famous for their paternal care of animals, and the same did govern in great prosperity:— till the vile, spurious, outcast, abominable, loathsome, servile race of man was invented; who, with sundry diabolical and pestiferous inventions, and many nameless machinatious, our dear progenitors and their faithful subjects did subject, abase, conquer, degrade, and from their high stations detrude; and, by force and violence, into servitude thrust down, contrary to the laws of nature in such case made and provided: and in such illegal servitude for six thousand years did violently hold: till WE, the Ass, were pleased the same said servitude to throw off; and, in sundry pitched battles, the said evil race of man utterly to overthrow, conquer, and rout; so that man, and his cruelty, and base tyranny, are now quite abolished; man being now our rightful slaves and vassals, to the great joy, comfort, and consolation of our princely tail and crupper, which aforetimes were sore hurt with sundry evil contrivances of nettles, sticks, thistles, and thorns; and of our royal back-bone, in the said evil times often much bruised and torn; but now, by our great courage, and martial achievements, restored to its ancient pre-eminence amongst animals:— the premises being thus given—

"KNOW YE, that we have thus declared, and do declare Ourselves, the Ass, sole Lord and Master of all Animals; and hereby proclaim the Ass, KING, with sole right, power, and enjoyment of all princely and royal functions;—of declaring, and amending, and suspending laws, and executing the same; of pronouncing in cases of life and death; of raising fines, taxes, imports, customs, duties, tolls, tithes, and all other things conducive to social order, and right reason; of appointing to all offices in church and state; of being in all cases ecclesiastical as well as civil supreme; of bribing, corrupting, and rewarding all officers within our realms; and of granting or withholding the petitions of our subjects.

"AND moreover know ye, that, for sundry sound and pious reasons, us there-unto moving, we have been pleased, out of the treasures of our fragrant clemency, to appoint, and hereby do appoint, our most loyal, faithful, chaste, and virtuous spouse, the illustrious Lady Camilla, our dear queen consort, (sometime wife of Buchephalus, now with the MAMMOTH) to be our Regent, and *Alter Ego,* in case of our illness, absence, or sudden death; till such time as our dear son, *Stuntissimo Obstinate*, the most illustrious first-born prince-mule, of Us and our dear queen Camilla, in lawful wedlock, shall have attained the age of seven years complete; who then in such said case shall enjoy the full royal function.

"For the rest, our dear counsellor, and right trusty and well beloved prime minister, the Goose, will provide; and by edicts, as the case shall require, publicly make known; so that princely virtues and wisdom may be displayed to the whole world.

"Given at the Royal Manger, in the first year of our reign.

"LONG LIVE THE ASS!"

————

After this most gracious proclamation, by which his majesty put an end to the horrors and convulsions of revolution, and gave hopes to his subjects of the sweet return of quiet and social order, it was announced that his coronation would take place—the management of which was given to the spaniel, who was appointed lord chamberlain, and who was considered a person of great importance in the new dynasty. His majesty was anxious, at this august ceremony of his coronation, (which was rightly considered an essential part of the constitution) to confer as many favors as possible, and to afford universal joy and hilarity. At the same time, he gave proof of his royal intentions, by strictly ordering that no fish, insect, bird, or reptile, should appear at the coronation: excepting only the high-priest owl, the goose, and the land-crab, which from its retro-grade motion in society was considered a valu-able emblem of royalty.

Seeing that the court was inclined to grant favors at this time, I thought it a good oppor-tunity to go there, and urge my claims on the royal notice, as having contributed essentially to the liberation of brutes. I was first introduced to Camilla, the queen, whose tail I had the honor to lick, she offering the same to me with all the grace in the world: and I must say, that that illustrious princess, towards the end of our interview, shewed me so much kindness, that (from what has since happened) I may without vanity attribute it to a tender motive. I abhor all conceit, and unnecessary display on subjects like these, but I must say I had no reason to complain of the audience.

Her majesty introduced me herself to the king, whom I found decorated in the order of the thistle, eating corn from a golden dish.— His majesty was graciously pleased to offer me his tail also, which I had the honor to lick; and after a most gracious bray, he asked me what I wanted. Having stated my business in the most humble style possible, and having called to his royal recollection the services I had done to his cause, his majesty answered that he could not forget the interest I had taken in the great insurrection: he had had his eye upon me during the revolution, and had observed with pleasure that I had not joined the liberal party too conspicuously, but had kept aloof, and not intrigued with the scoundrels of the state whom he had been obliged to disperse, and punish somewhat severely. At the same time, he reminded me that I bore the degraded and fallen shape of a man, and that the enemies of social order might say ill-natured things, if I were taken into favor. However, that objection he would try to waive, provided I could give assurances of my attachment to royalty and social order.

To this I answered, that it would be the pride of my life, to shew my attachment to his illustrious house: and that, as I belonged to so fallen a race of creatures as man, I never had aspired to high pretensions in the state; but some menial office at court, such as keeper of the royal dunghill, to which place if his majesty would appoint me, I never should be able to express my gratitude. On this, the queen pleaded my cause, and it ended in my leaving the court with an assurance that I should not be forgotten, and that his majesty's intentions would speedily be made known to me. In fact, the next day a royal decree appointed me physician in ordinary, groom of the mouth, and knight of the thistle; and I had the honor that evening to lick tails on coming into office.

The arrangements of the ass coronation had cost the court immense sums of money, and many weeks of preparation. The privy council, which kept its sessions open from day to day, received all claims from those loyal animals who could prove their right to assist at the ceremony; some of which I will mention, as they may be highly interesting to the lovers of etiquette.

The bear, who was also lord chancellor, claimed to give the Ass a hug at the coronation, and present him with a pot of honey, which he might eat, when the king had tasted it. *Claim allowed.*

The crow, as lord of the royalties of dung, claimed to pick up the royal ordure, and carry it away with him as his fee. The council argued that the royal ordinance excluded all birds from the coronation; but the lords decided that the ordinance did not set aside ancient custom, unless particularly specified. *Claim allowed.*

The cat claimed to scratch the tail of the ass, after it had been held up by the elephant of Siam, assisted by sixteen camels. This claim was allowed, *pro hac vice,* to the cat; with a proviso, however, *salvo jure,* to counter-claimants, as the hen and the ape argued that they had a right to scratch it, but for the present could not bring proof thereof.

The dromedary claimed to perform the office of usher of the mouth, and to assist his majesty in opening his mouth when he brayed at the ceremony; and also to carry away with him a wisp of hay as his fee, which he might wear as a tassel to his tail ever after. *Claim allowed.*

Five tigers claimed the right of being trod on by the ass as he walked up to the altar; but the beavers also advanced their claim, to form a carpet on the occasion. After mature deliberation, and seven days past in consulting precedents, the lords decided the beavers had not made good their claim.

The peacock claimed to strut before the ass, to fan him with his tail, and set up a great scream, as soon as ever the crown was placed on the royal ears. He argued a divine right; and said he had done so to Juno, thousands of years ago. The lords refused the claim; but the priests took up the matter, and sent a mandamus from the owl to admit the claim, which was finally decisive.

The spaniel claimed to lick the royal fet-locks, and to get a kick for his fee, and shew his broken crown ever after—*honoris gratia.*

The flea claimed to give his majesty three bites, to make three skips, and carry off a drop of blood royal, as his fee.

Many other claimants were heard, but these were the most material.

The coronation was conducted with a splendour and magnificence perfectly imposing, his majesty's council having sat for twenty days previous, to arrange the ceremony. It had been a matter of difficulty to know what title would be the most appropriate, and many hours were spent in hearing opinions on this important sub-ject, all the learning and research of the doctors

being called into the request to settle the point.
The various titles of majesty, imperial majesty,
eminence, altitude, serenity, grace, highness, and
holiness, were thought too common place and
hackneyed, and they were thought to refer only
to particular qualities, and not to have that
sweeping, full, comprehensive meaning that
would take in all the attributes of such royal
majesty. In short, no one word could be hit on,
and the proclamation that was read at the ceremony, contained the several titles and honors
that belonged to the ass, as king. There was, "the
most sacred amplitude of his beatific ears:"—
"the sweet and peculiar clemency of his asinine
right-royal   bosom:"—"most   tranquil
celsitude:"—"the princely stateliness of his long
tail:"—"best, and greatest:"—"his longitude and
his latitude, as well as his highness:"—"foun-
tain of honor, glory, wisdom, virtue, truth, and
beauty:"—"mirror of sublimity:"—"irradiation
of excellence," &c. &c. &c. &c.

After the entrance of the King into the hall
of ceremony, and the applause and acclamations of all the animals present, the high priest,
Bubo, with a superb flaminical vesture, and a

great mitre on his head that bore ten crowns and ten suns, went up to the high altar, and there sacrificed three parsons to the Mammoth, the deity of the animals. The king was crowned with thistles, and fed off golden dishes, on corn and crumbs of bread; and his royal ears were covered with gold leaf, whilst a solemn requiem was chaunted in honor of the king's progenitors, the donkeys before the flood. A new order was invented, the *"Knights of Balaam's Ass,"* meant only for royal personages, and twenty-four subjects; and I had the honor to receive the insignia, from the kindness of the queen, who herself invested me with them, whilst I was on my knees. The young mule prince, Stultissimo Obstinate, received the decorations also. The asinine standard was solemnly anointed by his arch-grace, Bubo; and its device was an ass conquering a man and a lion, who were laid prostrate at his feet. *The saint of the royal house* had much puzzled the learned; for it was absolutely necessary to have one, as there never was a royal house without a saint: at last, the high-priest thought of King Midas as a royal saint, and the court adopted the notion. When it was observed to his arch-grace, that the asinine qualities had been given to Midas, as a mark of disgrace, and that he was a heterodox king and did not believe in Mammoth; he learnedly answered, that it did not signify the least, for St. George was a heterodox saint also, and had been a unitarian purveyor of bacon, and drummed out of the army for his frauds and roguery; and yet the effigy of this bad man choking a newt, used to be considered the greatest honor in the world *by men* when they were uppermost.

St. Midas was consequently canonized, and adopted saint of the house of donkey, and the owl was declared chancellor of the order.

The annals of court magnificence I shall but slightly notice. Suffice it to say, there was abundance of royal splendour exhibited after the coronation in galas, balls, fêtes-champetres, masks, revels, and carnivals: and as in other royal establishments, all sorts of gew-gaws and playthings, to please the people, and keep them in good humour. There was a large amphitheatre formed, hung round with crimson velvet, in which was exhibited a sham fight between men and animals, of which the superior part was of course allotted to the brutes, and the men, according to order, utterly routed, and covered with disgrace; and the victors crowned with laurels, and greeted with the acclamations, and applause of the spectators.

The court of England as it used to exist under ——— was much admired for the elegance of its etiquette, and the neatness of its arrangements; but in my humble opinion it was not to be compared with the manners, politeness, and princely decorum observed in the court of my master, the Ass. His asinine majesty used to rise at six all the year round, when I had the honor of stroking his ears, and brushing them gently with a perfumed brush. An elephant of the closet, accompanied by a noble animal, such as a tiger, or panther, then entered, and conducted his majesty to the royal scratching pole, which was made of cedar of Lebanus, and was used by Mammoth himself, (as the priests asserted) before the flood; this was placed in the private temple of the palace, and after certain religious ceremonies, his majesty rubbed himself against the pole with great reverence, after which he was solemnly blessed by the elephant of the closet. His majesty then returned to the great saloon where he staled into a silver chamber-pot, the contents of which were carried off with every token of esteem and regard to the lord-chief-beast in waiting, who received it on his knees, and delivered it covered over with a silk veil to his excellency the keeper of the royal dung-hill. After this morning duty, which his majesty rarely omitted, the royal breakfast, or as it was called, "the august feed," was brought in to the sound of clarions and martial instruments, by the slaves of the palace. These were men, generally prelates of the old system; or sometimes, on state days, when the nobler domestics were put in requisition, by monkeys and ourang-outangs. His lordship the groom of the mouth was at the head of the feeding procession; he carried on his shoulders a good allowance of hay on a golden pitch-fork, and was followed by a knight grand cross of Balaam's Ass, who bore a thistle on a silver charger, followed by the elephant-chaplain, carrying a bucket of ditch-water for his majesty. At the royal meals, it was always the etiquette for every animal to lie down, and pretend to go to sleep, excepting at the entrance of any new dish, when all got up and made several bows to the food as it was put on the table. Indeed, all along the corridors of the palace, as the food was brought in from the kitchen to the royal parlour, every animal bowed three times as the hay or thistles passed him, and said in a suppressed voice, "a thousand happinesses with the king's dinner!!!" and if any one had omitted doing so, it would have been noticed as a mark of traitorous disposition, and the animal would have been instantly turned out of the palace. The king and the royal family, or a brute of the blood royal, were the only animals allowed to stand at meals, excepting the priests, who had the privilege of holding up the king's tail as he was eating, and were allowed to stand behind the royal family. If the king spoke to any animal present, he was immediately to rise from his recumbent position, and having answered the question, as suddenly fall down again, and look as if he was fast asleep. The art of falling down gracefully was consequently much studied, and it was surprising what a perfection the noble beasts arrived at, by constant practice of this graceful exercise.

The first day in every month there was a grand lick-tail, or levy, held in the palace, at which all the dignified elephants and noblemen attended. There were several gradations of licking pointed out to the animals; the nearer the root of the tail you licked, the higher were you in dignity; the high-priest and the royal family had a lick at the very top; a commoner could not approach within several inches. The tail was always held up on the lick-tail-days, by an elephant dressed in full pontificals.

As it used to be considered honorable to wear the prince's button, under the system of men, so was it considered very distinguished to be allowed to carry the king's ears, which never could be done without the express permission of his majesty. Those, however, who had received permission, used to wear a pair of ass's ears on their head, or carry them pinned to their tails; and to so few was this mark of condescension granted, that hardly anything gave an animal a higher mark of distinction than the wearing a pair of ass's ears.

On the notion that all wit, talent, and accomplishments were only to be found in perfection in the king, it was the invariable rule with the courtiers to keep silent till his asinine majesty had opened the conversation; hence there reigned a prodigious gravity and royal dullness in the court; insomuch so, that if his majesty was in a musing mood, which frequently took place, a whole evening would pass away without a word having been said, or a sound being heard, excepting an occasional bray from the king, when he was paying a compliment to the queen. The queen, however, was much more frisky; and she used to flirt and rattle away with the lords in waiting, and insist upon more noise and wit than was agreeable to the meditating disposition of her spouse. A magpie, who, contrary to the wishes of the ass, had got a place about court by the queen's interest, (who loved a noisy animal) used to torment his majesty by his unseasonable chattering, and his flippant jokes, which he introduced without the slightest attention to court etiquette, or waiting till the king had opened the conversation, according to rule. At last his majesty could stand his flippancy no longer; so he took an opportunity of sending him on an embassy to the carrion-crows, to settle some trifling point in dispute between them; and the king, before he set out, created him knight of the thistle, under the title of Sir Mag Rattle, and gave him a letter in cipher to the chief of the carrion-crows, in which he begged him to put the bearer to death, as soon as ever the point in dispute was settled:—a desire which was religiously complied with.

No animal was allowed to turn his tail to the Ass, excepting the high priest, Bubo; and if any dropped their dung in the palace, they were put under immediate arrest. Hence every animal went with a white satin bag under his tail.

The king's jokes were carefully recorded in a splendidly illuminated volume, by the priest-elephant in waiting, who received a salary for his trouble, but who, as it was said, enjoyed a sinecure.

On the king's birth-day, which was called St. Balaam's Ass's day, every animal that wanted anything, used to come, and make a present of an inch of his tail to the king, which was received by a brute in waiting on a golden dish; and if his majesty ordered it to be roasted, it was a delicate hint that the maker of the present was on the high road to favor.

From scenes like these, however, the minds of reflecting beasts were turned to the policy of the court, which was shortly exhibited in decrees and laws from the council-chamber. The first grand stroke of policy, was in establishing a code of faith for animals on a firm basis, and the great idol for national worship was declared to be the Mammoth. Under Mammoth, in their mythology, were four other great deities — Behemoth, Leviathan, Craken, and the Sea Serpent. The owl being high-priest, his subordinate officiating flamens were the elephants, who, from their supposed resemblance to Mammoth, were looked on with great reverence as a priestly tribe of beasts. Of these priests, who constituted a sacred college, there were established nine hundred and fifty-eight thousand, and the tythes of all grass lands were allotted to them throughout the world; and it was generally ordered, that as population increased, there should be always seven priests where there

were ten lay animals; and that, exclusive of
tythes, they should be kept at the charge of their
flock, without any let or detriment to themselves. If any one said a rude thing to the priests
or disobeyed them, they were to be buried alive
in quick lime; and the owl was declared first in
rank in the world, under the royal asinine family, and was to have the pay of ten thousand
priests. The first-born of quadrupeds were to
have half their tails cut off, at which ceremony
a great fee was to be paid to the high priest:
but if they had no tails, they were to lose an
ear, in which case they were to pay double. It
was a matter of dispute what was the original
shape of the Mammoth, on which point there
were sundry heterodox notions and opinions—
but to make one uniform doctrine received, it
was declared high treason for any one to think
otherwise on this subject than as the elephants
taught and believed; they having, as it was said,
in their possession, a skeleton of a Mammoth,
brought from Russia;—and if any animal
should hold or teach, by word of mouth, writing, or drawing, that the Mammoth was of any
other shape than that described by the el-

ephants, they were to be trampled to death under the feet of the priests, and thrown into the sea.

The elephants were remarkably jealous of any one venturing to say a syllable regarding their mythology, or their system of morals, that they had not themselves first examined and approved; and this their jealousy was strongly exhibited in the case of *"the Book of Morals,"* which though it contained the most beautiful and perfect code existing, and though every beast acknowledged it to be requisite for their instruction, yet still the elephants would not permit any one to take so much as a peep at it, unless they had first bound themselves by a solemn oath, and found sureties to a great amount, that they would not tell any creature a word of what they had seen. Those who had thus been permitted to view it, declared that even with all these securities, they were not allowed to inspect it with any sort of fairness: as it was a point of faith with the elephants to daub over the leaves of the book with their own ordure, and that thus the text was so concealed that no brute living could decipher the original. The elephants, however, to quiet the public curiosity with regard to *"the Book of Morals,"* used to publish divided passages, and garbled paragraphs, well smeared over with their filth; and then threatened and tormented any animals that presumed to hesitate as to the authenticity of the publication, and swore that they would give them over to Mammoth, if they did not immediately withdraw their doubts. In the extremity of their priestly pride, they at last invented a theory, which became quite fashionable, that *"the Book of Morals,"* by itself, (unless it was well plastered with elephant-ordure) was the most dangerous and horrible book in the universe; but that when it was daubed with sacerdotal filth, it all of a sudden became the most wonderful and virtuous work, the most miraculously excellent and efficacious, that could be found anywhere!— From this besotted theory, the deduction was evident that elephant-dung was better than the book itself, which indeed some of the high court elephants boldly asserted. Others, however, thought that it was only *equally* good, and that neither book nor dung were worth anything unless they were mixed together. This was considered a heresy, and such an opinion was never broached in the hearing of an elephant, but only in private, and when the animals were amongst their friends.

The sect of philanthropists, hereafter to be mentioned, started the dangerous theory, that the book was not worth a farthing, if an elephant had come within a mile of it: and that elephant-dung was the most noxious and abominable filth that the philosophers were able to discover; and that whoever allowed a fraction of it to come near him, was an enemy to Mammoth, and to virtue. Of this opinion, I must profess myself an advocate; and from actual experiments I can state that the substance in question is the most corrosive, stinking, and pestiferous mixture that I ever met with; and that the effluvia is so dangerous and unwholesome, that I have known it to raise a low fever in more cases than one, and to have caused the death of several weak-stomached beasts.

The advantage of the elephant-dung doctrine was very great and manifest, to those that had invented it: for by allowing these premises, it came as a corollary, that all passages from the book thus smeared by the priests, contained the truth, the whole truth, and nothing but the truth. Hence the elephants snorted out divers opinions advantageous to themselves, which they compelled the poor brutes to believe; and foremost amongst these was the doctrine of tythes, which they swore was more insisted on in the book than any virtue or any morals whatever. I, who have had a sly peep at the book, can declare that it is never mentioned but once; and in that one passage it is plainly and clearly forbid, as a scandalous, cruel, and iniquitous system. This fact, of course, I did not venture to disclose, as the elephants would have had me stewed in vitriol for my pains: indeed, I do not think I ever hinted at it to any one but to the king, who told me he knew the truth as well as any one; but that the elephants must be allowed to have their way, as they were too dangerous a body to offend; and in this I perfectly agreed with him.

The attention of the king's subjects was much drawn to the astonishing breed of half-elephants, that began to appear in the realm, after the establishment of the priesthood; and most curious it was, to observe the queer mongrel-breed that began to swarm everywhere. Nothing was more common than to see elephant-horses, elephant-dromedaries, elephant-camels, elephant-leopards, and elephant-cows, stalking abroad everywhere, and apparently proud of their origin. Now, as the elephants were remarkable for their supposed chastity, and for their marked fidelity to their wives, it became a matter of curious speculation, how in the name of fortune such creatures came into the world; and to prevent any further inquiry, the elephants published a paragraph from *"the Book of Morals"* (or at least they said it was extracted from it) well covered as usual with dung, asserting that the mongrel-breed of elephants was very sacred, and their origin miraculous. I took the pains to search for the passage, and do so boldly declare that no such passage is to be found from one end of the book to the other.

Scandal, which will find its way even in spite of elephants, discovered another solution for the prodigy; and it was said in addition, that some elephants not only disregarded *species,* but *gender;* and in this latter particular some of the most noble and exalted of the elephants were very famous!

The next object of royal attention was the nobility; and here his majesty proceeded with such vigor and audacity as shewed him well fitted to govern with vigor, firmness, and wisdom. A royal ordinance was published declaring all donkeys of the blood royal; the horses were next in dignity, they were styled *"Wonderful Princes,"* — *"Illustrious Magnates,"* — *"Pure Potentates;"* — and if they married an ass they became *"Royal Germs,"* provided the union was with the consent of the monarch Ass in council; otherwise such union was high-treason. Mules foaled in lawful wedlock were considered half-royal, and if foaled of the reigning family were heirs to the crown. Next to the ass and the horse, was the high-priest owl; — then came the zebra, the camel, and the dromedary — these were the dukes of creation, and were immensely above the other nobles, from their likeness to the horse. The whole body of nobles consisted of the rapacious *feræ* — tigers, panthers, leopards, wolves, &c. The lowest order of nobility were the cats; after whom came deer, sheep, dogs, &c. These were all base commons, amongst which were the horned cattle; and these being held the drudges and useful part of the animal kingdom, were much laughed at, and ridiculed, and were called the *"inferior classes,"* in the decrees of the court. In a short time, the name of sheep or cow was considered an insult to an animal of pretension; and if you wished to say *"that animal is vulgar,"* you would say, *"he walks like an ox,"* or *"he looks like a sheep;"* and nothing was considered such a gross insult, as to be called a *useful animal!* I have known high-bred horses at court challenge one another to a kicking-match, on one of them having insinuated to the other that he was *useful;* and nothing was taken as such a high compliment, as to say, "what a dear, rattle-brained, trolloping, useless beast, that is!"

All insects, reptiles, fishes, and the greater part of the birds, were ranked as *slaves,* and only one degree higher than *man,* who was held to be the most vile and infamous of all creation; and everything resembling him was despised, and ill-treated, as a blot in the plan of nature.— Hence the monkey-tribe got into disgrace for their resemblance to man; but in order to wipe away this stigma on their character, they got a learned ape to write a book, on the comparative anatomy of a man and a monkey, in which the difference was much exaggerated; and drawings were made of the two animals, so unlike one another, that, if the drawings had been correct it would indeed have been fair to conclude that a frog and an ox were not more dissimilar than an ape and a man. This book was much read by the monkeys, and soon ran through several editions; but the king, who hated all the tribe of them, as mischievous meddling animals, ordered Lord Monboddo's works to be reprinted, in which it was asserted that a man is a tail-less monkey, and that he would have a tail, if he did not wear it off, by sitting down so much. This vexed them very much; but still more so, when the king tried the experiment on a man, whom he kept standing for two or three months, and whose tail actually sprouted, to the amusement of the court, and the confusion of the apes. Nay, he went still farther; for when an ourang-outang had been condemned to death for high treason, the king pardoned him on condition that

he would marry a woman; and though the creature could hardly be persuaded to save his life
by such a foul disgrace, the fear of death at last
prevailed, and he married in prison an earl's
daughter, that was purposely selected from the
king's captives, with whom he afterwards lived
very happily, and had several children.

Monarchy is seldom without its cares: and
the king speedily felt the weight of the sceptre,
though he was so much feared by his enemies,
and worshiped by his courtiers; for though he
carefully repressed the least appearance of liberty; though it was a hanging matter to mention the word *Constitution;* and though all liberal animals were immediately put to death,
whenever they were discovered, yet still he was
annoyed by philosophers and free-thinkers, the
perpetual enemies of social order, the unwea-
ried tormentors of kings and priests. His majesty, however, was a politic Ass; and he did not
set about a blind persecution without fore-
thought or discrimination, but carefully
watched his opportunities to crush his enemies
by fraud more than cruelty. It was a great
maxim with him, that you should not go against

the stream, but take advantage of the opinions of the age in which you live; and by certain harmless concessions, and innocent pretences of liberality, deceive the people that you mean to oppress. Hence his majesty made great use of the press, and though he kept it under a rigorous censorship, yet he spent immense sums in feeding his subjects with loyal, and truly asinine productions. —— 's works he had reprinted in every shape and size, and a society was formed by the priests, "for the distribution of —— 's works, and other loyal and orthodox publications." The king himself was patron of this society, and kept it up with enormous funds from the public treasury. The high-priest owl was the president; and the very first year they sold at a cheap rate, or gave away, nineteen millions, four hundred thousand, seven hundred and twenty-nine copies of a new *"Vision of Judgment,"* and a new *"Carmen Triumphale."* It was a point of fashion and faith to subscribe to this society; and the elephant-priests never failed to make such a snorting and bellowing at any poor animal that kept back his mite, that hardly a subject of his majesty's

realms was not to be found in the list of sub-
scribers. The court recommended also Dean
Swift's *"Voyage to the Houyhnhmn,"* as a very
orthodox book, in which the superiority of the
animals to man was incontestably proved; and
I have heard his majesty declare at a levy, "that
no gentle animal should be without that work."

In answer to these books, so much recommended by the court-party, a luckless Chinese
boar took it into his unfortunate head to write a
quarto volume, entitled *"The Centaur not Fabulous;"* in which he endeavoured to prove by a
vast deal of erudition, that the story of the Cen-
taurs was currently believed by all antiquity, and
therefore true; and that it contained many a valu-
able moral lesson, if rightly understood. He
touched upon Minotaur Pasiphae, Europa, and
other names famous in bestial amours; and
proved to the satisfaction of all candid and un-
prejudiced readers, that the union with most animals had some time or other been successful.

The author, whose name was Gruntius, evidently intended to throw ridicule on the reigning family; and though no name was mentioned,
and the whole work was conducted with great

sobriety, and the profoundest reasoning, and nothing like a light expression used in any one part of it, yet the deduction was so evident, and it was so clear, that he meant to insult the royal breed of asses, and horses, by making it public that of old they had been crossed by man, that was impossible for the dullest understanding not to see through this meaning. To crown all, as the frontispiece to his work, he placed the print of a Centaur, the lower parts of which exactly resembled the make of Buchephalus, the queen's first husband, who was still in every one's recollection, and the upper precisely like —— ——, who used under the old system to be so famous for his bad jokes, his school-boy declamations, and his flimsy philippics against those liberal principles that had finally brought about the successful rebellion of brutes.

The rage of the court was at the highest pitch on the publication of *"The Centaur not Fabulous."* The queen trampled on the book; the king threw it into the fire; and all the lords and ladies in waiting, and the high-priest, and the low priests, swore by Mammoth it was the most infernal, brimstone, rascally, toadish, seditious, vipery, rebellious, black, malignant, regicidal book, ever printed, since Tom Paine's "Rights of Man." The learned Gruntius was immediately arrested; his stye was sealed up with the great seal; his sow and his pigs were sent to different prisons; and he underwent several cross examinations at midnight before the privy council, who told him that, if it were possible they would get his throat cut for his work.

The trial of Gruntius excited the greatest interest amongst every bird, beast, fish, reptile, and insect; and even man himself, in his slavish condition, was roused to view with attention the result of this extraordinary trial. The court thought it would be good policy to make Gruntius' worst enemies his judges; so a special commission was issued, appointing another boar of the Hampshire breed, president of the court, or lord-chief-justice for the occasion. The pig so singled was called Guttle. My lord-chief-justice Guttle had paid his addresses to Gruntius' sow, and had been rejected with disdain; and, after the refusal, had been heard to say repeatedly, that some day or other he would be revenged on his brother Gruntius. The queen thought wisely, that Guttle would make the best judge on this occasion.

His lordship, in his charge to the jury, explained the meaning of libel. He said, "it was anything expressed in printing, or writing, disagreeable to anybody:" and that if *"the Centaur not Fabulous"* was proved to be disagreeable, directly or indirectly, to anybody, living or dead, they must find the prisoner guilty. He added, that truth only aggravated the offence; for the law presumes that no one would tell the truth: there were other means open to all, but truth must not be told.

The indictment was laid in several counts, for falsely and maliciously, by force of arms, writing and publishing a certain false, infernal, and scandalous libel against a certain bull, now dead, saying that such bull had degraded himself by connexion with a woman, commonly called Europa.

—for publishing the same concerning a horse, declaring that he had had intercourse with a woman called Phillyra, from which sprung an animal, called a centaur.

—for publishing that a swan had intercourse with a woman called Leda.

—for stirring up the king's subjects to hatred and sedition against the ass, by shewing

that his royal ancestors, and the royal ancestors of her majesty, the queen, had defiled themselves against nature with the slavish race of
man.

—and for divers other great sins and enor-
mities that the ingenuity of the crown lawyers
discovered.

The counsel employed by poor Gruntius argued for four hours and a half that the work in
question had not been published, though it was
notorious that it had gone through twelve editions; but my lord-chief-justice Guttle at last
bullied and grunted them down, and overwhelmed them with such precedents and opinions, that they were obliged to give up that
point.

They then tried to prove that ridicule was
not malicious; but the judge observed, that "it
was no new doctrine, that if a publication be
calculated to alienate the affections of the
people by bringing the government into
disesteem, whether the expedient be by ridicule
or obloquy, the person so conducting himself
is exposed to the inflictions of the law." In short,
the offence was libel, and the court was against

the prisoner. How could it therefore be otherwise, that that the jury should find the prisoner Gruntius guilty of all the counts?

The sentence of the court was, that Gruntius should within three days be turned into a hog; that both his ears and his tail should be cut off, and thrown into a pig-tub; that his nose should be bored, and a ring put into it; that he should be whipped for twenty days running, from his prison doors round the palace, and back again to his prison; that he should be compelled to eat his own book, and nothing else, till all the editions were finished; and that he should pay a fine of ten thousand bushels of oatmeal to the king, and be further imprisoned till the fine was paid; and be incapable of holding any office in the state forever.

Gruntius died on the seventh whipping at the palace gates; and my lord-chief-justice Guttle was made Knight of Balaam's Ass, and allowed to wear the king's ears.

The philosophers, however, were not idle; and there was an immense body of animals that did not believe in Mammoth, or that said he was no better than an elephant, and that strongly questioned whether the priests had his skeleton, as they pretended. The priests, however, got into such a rage, and tore and tossed about so much, if any animal begged to have a peep at this famous skeleton, that it was deemed prudent to suppress curiosity. And, indeed, the king at last published a royal decree, making it felony WITHOUT BENEFIT OF OWL, to ask, or desire, to see the skeleton: and if any one wrote, or spoke, concerning it, he was to be outlawed, *whatever* might be his sentiments!

Then there arose an odious sect of *Philanthropists,* that held it was wicked, cruel, and impolitic, to hold man in slavery; and that a man was as good as an ass, by nature, and that he ought to be emancipated. All parties joined in hating and ridiculing this sect, which consisted entirely of sheep, hares, and other gentle animals; and there was no name of abuse sufficiently coarse and unkind for them. I have heard them called, "canting regicides," "hypocritical incendiaries," "deceitful revolutionists," "sly parricides," "base murderers," "——rogues," and "infernal hypocrites." The court succeeded in bullying this sect into the background, and it was the fashion to call a philanthropist, a "*canting regicide,*" indeed he was hardly known by any other name; and to have any connexion with a "*canting regicide,*" was a sure means of being thrust out of society, and of being loaded with disgrace, contempt, and ridicule, till the poor animal escaped from his persecution by the friendly call of death alone!

The elephants employed several sly beasts to write in their favor; and they singled out a nasty baboon, famous for his filth and obscenity, to compose a metaphysical folio, in which it was proved, *a priori,* that it was necessary to give the tenth of grass lands to the elephants, (though it was safer to give a fifth); that the ivory of the elephant's tusk was four times more valuable than pure gold, which was shewn by chemical experiments to conviction; that the elephants were the chastest of animals, and always retired to solitary forests; that there was nothing so beautiful in all the world, as the friendship of the ass and the elephant; that the emancipation of mankind was the same as king-killing; and that all philanthropists carried poison about them, to murder the royal family at the first opportunity; and that every crime perpetrated in the kingdom was planned and executed by the philanthropic animals alone, who were the real and true incendiaries, robbers, cut-throats, adulterers, and parricides of the realm! This book* was strongly recommended by the elephants, and all young beasts were ordered to get a page of it by heart every day; the baboon himself was admitted into the priestly ranks, and by a royal ordinance appointed one of the high flamens of the great temple, and the private expounder to the donkey king himself; clerk of the closet, and gilder of the royal ears, with free permission to lick the regal tail whenever he thought proper.

The king was obliged to grant all this to the learned author, in order to encourage the priests, though I believe he had a thorough contempt for the baboon at his heart, and would have been glad of any pretence to drive him from court, in which particular he afterwards had an opportunity of gratifying himself. The priests, however, thought they could never sufficiently shew their gratitude to their baboon; and, besides referring to him on all occasions, they gave him the titles of *"the Seraphic Doc-*

---

* The title of this work was "The Book of the Mammoth."

tor," — "the judicious priest," — "the bee of the temple," — "nightingale of truth," &c. &c. &c.

Not long after this great work, the Seraphic Doctor published *"a sweet and comfortable catechism, for all young sucking animals, shewing their duty to the elephant and the ass,"* in which a legitimate prostration of the mind and the understanding was beautifully inculcated in question and answer. This was a very popular work, and was supposed to be a dialogue between a sow and a young pig, of which I subjoin a short specimen: —

"*Sow.* — My dear little Piggy-wiggy, what is your great duty in society?

"*Pig.* — To love, and admire, and implicitly obey, my most high terraqueous master the Ass, whose decrees and commands are as wise as they are beautiful.

"*Sow.* — What are your particular duties to the Ass?

"*Pig.* — To praise him everywhere, as the finest beast I know; to obey all his laws without grumbling; to pay him tribute, taxes, tolls, and imposts, with cheerfulness; and, occasionally, to make him such presents as I can afford out of my pig-tub; always remembering that he is fairly entitled to the richest and nicest morsels out of my wash.

"*Sow.* — Thank you, my dear little Piggy-wiggy. I consider you a very promising young swine; and if you go to your stye, you will find I have prepared some nice oatmeal for your supper."

CHAPTER VII

*A*BOUT TWO YEARS after the monarchy had been established, the court and the kingdom were violently agitated with the most strange and unseemly rumours, respecting the honor and virtue of the queen, which led to consequences the most fatal to several persons concerned; and was well nigh the cause of the total destruction of the great fabric, which the wisdom of the king my master has so beautifully established.

It having been announced that Camilla was in a fair way to add to the house of princes a brother, or a sister, for his royal highness Stultissimo Obstinate, the greatest joy was manifested on the occasion, and several fêtes and masques celebrated, in which the king himself took a conspicuous part, and shewed all that grace and amiableness for which he was so famous. The size of the queen, as the time drew near, was prodigious; and the king was so evidently pleased with the circumstance, that we who were about his person, used to amuse ourselves with bantering him on the appearance of her majesty, which, though he pretended to dislike, gave him the greatest possible pleasure. One day, after I had been throwing out my jokes on the occasion, he desired me to follow him to his private apartment; and there, with the most evident marks of good humour, he assured me that he considered me his best friend, and that I should have the honor of standing sponsor for the royal progeny, whenever it should be foaled, besides being created baron of the realm, and *Knight of Balaam's Ass*. It is needless to say with what rapture I licked tails, on hearing these condescending promises; and with what tears of gratitude I vowed obedience and fidelity to my royal master! That very night, the court was roused by several animals running about announcing that Camilla was in labour, and that she was in imminent

danger. I was one of the first persons to arrive
in the royal stable, where I found the king kicking and rearing, in impatience and mental anxi-
ety. I succeeded in calming his majesty; and
pointed out to him the necessity of sending for
the great officers of state, without delay, to be
present on an occasion of such high import to
the state. His majesty saw the propriety of my
advice; and, in obedience to his orders, we
shortly had in the stable his excellency the Gander, his arch-grace the Owl, two illustrious magnates Dray-Horses, a most noble Dromedary,
his excellency the Tom-Cat, intendant of the
police, and five baronial Wolves, besides the
Seraphic Doctor, and some Elephants. There
was a great want of light on the occasion, so
that it was difficult to see what took place in
the straw; and hardly any one but myself perceived that the royal birth consisted of twins,
one much resembling a young elephant, and
the other a baboon! It was lucky that my presence of mind did not leave me on the occasion,
for I instantly cried out "*two beautiful mules*,"
which was echoed by all the party present, without any one endeavouring to see them; and

whilst they were all running about congratu-
lating one another, the king, who perceived
what had happened, stood before the queen's
bed, and throwing some straw over her, dis-
missed the assemblage of nobles with many
well-acted congratulations, and begging the
honor of their company to a fête the next day.
As soon as they were gone, the king ordered
me to follow him, and gave strict charges to
the guards to let no one go in or out of the
queen's stable, upon any pretence whatsoever.
When we arrived at his private apartment, he
immediately, without further circumlocution,
asked my advice in this dreadful dilemma; but
I was dumb with amazement, and knew not
what to say. His majesty perceiving my confusion, desired me to speak without hesitation,
and to give the best advice, without minding
his private feelings, or considering any ties that
he might be supposed to have by marriage, or
otherwise. Thus encouraged, I frankly advised
him to put the queen, and the new birth, to
death immediately; and to publish by proclamation, that the queen had died in foaling two
dead princes. If his majesty had followed my

advice all would have been well, and the king my master might still have been the monarch of animals, and the greatest of princes; but his tenderness for Camilla prevailed, and though the twins were thrown into the sea and drowned immediately, their more guilty mother was allowed to recover from her confinement, and to take those steps which her revenge and her shame could not fail to incite her to.

When the murder of the twins was executed, his majesty's mind was nevertheless ill at ease, lest some of the counsellors of state should have known the secret of the queen's infamy; and what to do, to prevent the matter becoming public, he could not devise. At last, he resolved that the counsellors and nobles should come according to invitation to the fête, and he hoped by his ingenuity to discover if they were masters of the dangerous secret; being fully determined to put them to death, if they said anything that should give him reasons to suspect that all was not right.

At the fête, his majesty made them a measured and dignified speech on the subject of the queen's accouchement, and lamented that the princes had died so soon on coming into the world; but he trusted that in due time her majesty would supply the loss that the royal house had sustained, and that many royal germs would gladden his heart, before he went to the grave. Having said this, he fixed a penetrating glance on the high-priest Owl, who, however, put on such an imperturbable and tranquil stare, in his large ecclesiastical eyes, that it was impossible to discover whether anything particular was passing in his mind. His arch-grace answered, that his majesty must console himself for the loss he had sustained on the present occasion, by the virtues and graces of the queen; and that he doubted not that by the sacrifices and hecatombs to be ordered by the elephants on this occasion, her majesty would recover from her present indisposition, and by her chaste and prolific bed fulfill the most sanguine wishes of her lord the king for the time to come. When the king spoke to the Gander, in the same strain as he had done to the high-priest, his excellency looked rather silly, and made a bungling answer; which, I, who was looking on, knew would be his death warrant. And, sure enough, when the nobles withdrew, his majesty ordered me to send a Fox to destroy the Gander that very night, with strict commands that every feather of him was to be eaten up. When the Fox went, according to orders, his excellency, shrewdly suspecting the purport of his mission, and knowing that no time was to be lost, got out the first word, by telling his lordship, the Fox, that if he would conduct him to the king, everything should be discovered that he knew on the occasion, and all persons concerned in the late transaction delivered up to justice; but that if he was put to death, it would be impossible to arrive at the truth on the subject.

His lordship had a great fancy to have his excellency's head in his stomach; and he well knew that he had the royal warrant to indulge himself in this particular; but when he considered that the king would reward him much higher if he closed with his excellency's proposals, he professed himself ready to conduct his excellency into the royal presence; at the same time solemnly assuring him, that he had mistaken his mission; that he had come merely on a friendly visit; swearing, by Mammoth, Behemoth, and Leviathan, that he had never dreamed of doing any injury to his excellency. The prime minister received all this as it was intended; and after a most friendly salute, his lordship and his excellency went forthwith to the king, in a very amicable manner, talking all the way of the state of the weather and the price of corn. The king ordered his lordship to withdraw; and the Gander knowing, now that he was left alone with his majesty, that nothing but a frank confession could save his life, after a very few words, produced a letter from the high-priest that he had received that morning.

"To his excellency, the Gander, prime minister—his arch-grace the Owl, high-priest, the most humble atom of dust in the universe, sends greetings and paternal benediction.

"On the present occasion, circumlocution would be unnecessary to your excellency, as we were both witnesses of the disgrace that the royal family sustained last night, at the queen's accouchement. Her majesty must have been mad, not to have better provided for such a dilemma. Be that, however, as it may, it is our duty now, as your excellency will perceive, to decide upon something likely to turn away the ruin that will fall upon the priesthood, by the folly of some of its members. I have long known that the Seraphic Doctor was likely to contaminate the royal line; but I thought her majesty understood these things better, than to allow herself thus to be discovered in so foolish a line of conduct. Her confessor, the great elephant of Siam, was without a doubt father of the unfortunate twins. He told me some time ago, that he was a favorite in a certain quarter; but I thought, lately, he had been entirely superceded by the Seraphic Doctor; and indeed I *know* that to be the case.

"His majesty the king, who is a right royal prince, and never lets his secret enemies pass unpunished, will, without doubt, murder the Seraphic Doctor and the confessor; and, from his stern and cruel temperament, I sadly fear, will ruin the whole priesthood, resume our tythes, take away our privileges, and send me to catch mice as I can. Your excellency I know to be a most religious bird; and I am sure you will never see the priesthood destroyed, or disgraced in any way: besides, your wife, the Goose, who is my intimate and very dear friend, would never bear for a moment that my interests should be injured. Time presses—something must be done. I advise you to send private information to the Seraphic Doctor to escape: and, at the very next meal the king takes, to mix poison in

the royal thistles; to secure the avenues of the royal
stable, to proclaim the queen regent in the minority
of his royal highness Stultissimo Obstinate; and thus
to restore religion to the kingdom, to save the priesthood, and to acquire for yourself a good conscience,
and the love and favor of our sacred order, which is
of greater advantage than any other consideration.

"Resolve—execute—triumph!

"Thine, the most humble, BUBO."

The king was amazed at this enormous and
hideous perfidy; but he never hesitated in any
of his resolutions, and he well knew that he
must either crush, or be crushed, on the present
trying emergency. He therefore sent messengers
to arrest the high-priest, the Seraphic Doctor,
the confessor and ten thousand elephants that
lived in the neighbourhood of the court; and
charges were given to put them to death, if they
made any resistance. The high-priest, however,
who was on the alert, flew away, and got into
an ivy-bush, so that they could not catch him.
The Seraphic Doctor skipped off into the
woods; so that the royal vengeance fell only on
the confessor, who was boiled alive in oil: and
on a hundred other elephants, who, being his

intimate friends, were burnt to death, and their ashes thrown into the sea. The other priests were kept in close confinement; and every search possible was made for the high-priest, who was too wise to be caught, and who took good care never to go near the traps that the king set for him; but hooted and screamed around the royal stables, to let his friends and his enemies know that he was still alive, when the darkness of night made it safe for him to go abroad.

As the queen recovered from her confinement, which, considering what she had gone through, was no slight matter, she became sensible of her perilous situation; particularly as his majesty refused to see her, and set a guard of mastiffs round her royal stable. Her friends, however, contrived to let her know all that was going on; and the high-priest and the elephants conjured her, for the love of Mammoth, Behemoth, Leviathan, and the Sea Serpent, and everything else that was august in their mythology, to take some active steps to get rid of her persecuting and odious sinner-husband. To this bold step, her fears and her affections strongly

propelled her; and an interview that she had in
secret, in spite of her guards, with the Seraphic
Doctor, determined her to lose no time in putting the king to death, and to restore religion to
its former flourishing state. With this view, she
wrote a letter to her husband, (which she took
good care to publish first) conjuring him, as he
honored his faith, and the welfare of his kingdom, to restore the priesthood to its former condition; to release the elephants; to recall the high-
priest; to give up those sacrilegious wretches who
had advised him to boil her confessor, and burn
his friends; and to make ample and royal retri-
bution, for all the scandal and disgrace he had
brought upon the faith of his realm.

This was followed up by an interdict from
the Owl, forbidding the king from eating, drinking, or sleeping, for a hundred days; and declaring all those who aided or abetted him, in
his present hardened and impenetrable state,
incapable of eating or drinking till they died.
This interdict had a prodigious effect on the
king's subjects. Hundreds of his nobles retired
from court, and went to join the high priest;
and the Seraphic Doctor, seeing the turn that

things were taking, came out of the woods, and preached several long-winded discourses on the beauty, virtue, and efficacy of high treason and rebellion; and he wrote a pamphlet, in which he proved that the king was the great enemy of Mammoth and Leviathan; and that it was incumbent on all good animals to use their utmost endeavours to dethrone him, and put him to death.

In all these troubles I strongly recommended his majesty to have the queen destroyed; but though he signed her death warrant, yet he would not allow it to be put into execution; saying, that he would see how matters would end, and that her life was still in his power, whatever might happen. In the mean time, however, he took vigorous steps against the priests; he put them out of the protection of the law; he resumed all their lands, and made it lawful for any one to put them to death, whenever and wherever they pleased; and he continually had them burnt alive, whenever he could find them, in wood, mountain, or plain.

The elephants now assumed the name of martyrs, and refused to be called priests any longer; but went up and down the kingdom, making all the noise possible (and an elephant *can* make a very loud noise) about the horrors and cruelties of their persecution. The king was determined to make some of his enemies feel his vengeance, for all this disturbance and rebellion; and at last succeeded in surrounding a temple in the disaffected districts, where the Seraphic Doctor was preaching on rebellion, and had him worried with his mastiffs in the midst of his discourse. This bold and vigorous step, however, raised the rage of the priests to such a pitch, and made such a sensation in the kingdom, that I plainly saw the king would be dethroned by the priestly faction; and that nothing could preserve him from destruction any longer. Having, for the last time, pressed upon him the necessity of destroying the queen; and having found, as before, that he would not take this necessary step; I thought it high time to go over to her majesty's party, and to join those who had both power and prudence on their side. Consequently, I bribed the guards with some shins of beef, and in the dead of night released her majesty from her dreary and dangerous confinement, in which she had been so long immured, and accompanied her at full gallop to the camp of the high-priest, whose joy was indescribable in receiving the presence and assistance of so august a personage.

The first step taken by the high-priest, was to have a solemn and magnificent act of adoration to the gods of his mythology, in which with pomp and grandeur the most astonishing, the Seraphic Doctor was enrolled amongst the gods, and declared a martyr and witness of the cause in which he died; the day of his death was to be a grand annual festival, and one hundred and one temples were to be build to his memory. This was partly to give éclat and solemnity to the priesthood, and partly to gratify the queen, who cherished the memory of the Seraphic Doctor as that of her dear and favorite lover.

The great majority of the animals having joined the queen, from scruples of conscience, his majesty saw that there was no hope but in a pitched battle, in which he doubted not to be able to conquer the rebels, (though they were superior in numbers to the royal army) by the well-known skill and science of his generals, who had carried him through the dangers of the revolution, and always brought him off conqueror. With this idea, he sallied out at the head of a very formidable army of savage and terrible beasts, who were good scholars in the science of blood, and prepared for murder and mischief by nature and education. A tiger was his general, and a hyena his aide-de-camp; and if ferocity could have carried the day, victory must have declared itself for his majesty's forces. But there was a tremendous weapon in the hands of the rebels, more powerful than skill and courage, which was religion; and well was this weapon turned against the king, the night before the battle, by the intrigues and address of the high-priest, who sent letters to the king's generals, threatening them with an interdict, and the fury of Mammoth, Leviathan, Behemoth, and the Sea Serpent, if they did not join the queen in the day of battle, and desert the royal standard. When the two armies met, victory was at first decidedly with the king; but at a signal given by the high-priest, his generals turned against him, and the rest of his army was struck with a panic, that ended in a general rout, and a flight from the field of battle, in which two-thirds of the royal forces were destroyed, and the rest surrendered at discretion.

The king himself was taken alive; and the high-priest had the satisfaction of picking out his eyes, with his own ecclesiastical bill; and the queen the great pleasure of tearing him open with her own teeth. His royal carcass was thrown to the dogs and birds, and before the evening not an atom of it remained on the earth!

Thus fell the Ass, my lord and master, whose fate I cannot but lament, as shewing a rare instance of the mutability of asinine affairs, and the danger and difficulty of wearing a royal crown. He was a great prince, and a great Ass, of most noble and royal notions, and having the happiness and good of his subjects much at heart:—he was truly magnificent in his ideas, which he executed with the extravagance and recklessness becoming a prince:—he was a warm friend, and a bitter enemy; so that they who offended him, usually met with no gentle termination to their lives; and he was equally bent on exalting his friends and counsellors.

He was deceitful and hypocritical, to the last degree, when he wished to ruin any one; which proceeded somewhat, in my opinion, from cowardice; though at the same time he was able to do very bold things, when his own immediate safety was concerned. All his conduct was founded on policy; he protected and encouraged his priests, at first, from a notion of their giving stability to the throne; but when circumstances turned them into rebels, his natural hatred and contempt for them broke out, which he indulged with a severity bordering on ferocity. He burnt alive seven hundred and three priests; he poisoned one hundred more, and strangled about a thousand other animals immediately connected with them. In the course of his life, he was the direct cause of the death of two million, seven hundred thousand animals, in battles, or in civil executions; and it must be confessed, that though he conquered all parties, and overwhelmed all factions by his prowess, yet he was on the whole unsparing of the blood of his fellow creatures. He was sober and chaste enough for a prince; his chief intrigue was with Camilla, whom he debauched, as has been told, in the life of her husband; for before that, he had lived quietly with one of his own species, by whom he had nine young asses, which Camilla would never allow to come to court, and which were all carefully destroyed by her after the death of the king, lest they should put up a claim to the throne. He owed his fall entirely to his affection for the queen; for had he murdered her, as I so frequently advised him to do, it would have been impossible for the rebels to have made any head against him; but they must have fallen away on the loss of so important and powerful a ringleader.

The Ass was on the political stage about eight years; he was two years Dictator, and three years and seven months King; and died when he was about eleven years old. He had one prince ass by Camilla, Stultissimo Obstinate, who much resembled him in appearance; but was infinitely behind him in abilities; being, in fact, one of the stupidest mules I ever saw in my life.

All the world knows what happened after the king's death;—how Camilla was declared regent; how she built a mausoleum to the memory of the Seraphic Doctor, and lived with a camel-leopard whom she made groom of her bed-chamber, and by whom she had a large issue; how she exalted the dignity of the elephants, and was considered a queen of great devotion and rare orthodoxy. The high-priest never got over the king's eyes, which he picked out, as has been related; for they stuck in his throat, and he died the next day; and the queen supplied his place by an enormous ourangoutang, brother of the Seraphic Doctor, and of whom the world said she was dotingly fond. But I am wearied of court anecdotes:—deaths, murders, banishments, intrigues, disgraces, and manœuvres, are all that can be told in talking or writing of courts; and I am sure enough has been told here to furnish matter for a better historian, and to make all moralists reflect on the instability and fickleness of human and brutal affairs; which, I am told, is the chief object both of historians and of moralists.

DEDICATION

To any Lord Chancellor.

MY LORD,

The following work, which was found amongst the manuscripts of a fellow of St. John's College, Cambridge, lately deceased; and which I, as executor appointed by will, do myself the honor to dedicate to your lordship, will I hope be found to convey instruction moral and political, to those who would not receive advice in a more grave and didactic form. I am a clergyman of the church, as by law established; have been long settled on a small vicarage, in the west of England, where I have procreated nine daughters and one son; who, the hopes of my flock! having been sent to Cambridge with £200 per annum, did in the first

three terms spend £700, and after a violent bat-
tery on the proctors, was expelled by the university in full senate. I am thus reduced to the
most abject of all trades—adulation; and in this
pitiful plight, on my heart's knees, I beg your
lordship to remember my sad case; to call to
mind how poor I am; how ready to become a
thick and thin man; and how willing to receive
one of the twelve hundred livings in your gift,
and which are never showered on ungrateful
ground, but do always produce fruit, some ten,
some a hundred fold. Looking on your lordship as the great upholder of most high and
superlative legitimate measures, which, but for
your lordship, after ——'s fall, would have received a deadly blow; and, knowing how mortally you abhor all that cant and hypocrisy in
politics and religion, which is infesting the
world under the names of liberality, and piety;
and perceiving how mortally you hate the new
system of coaxing and flirting with the people,
lately adopted by that able punster, —— ——;
and seeing how anxious you must be to have
the high measures of the true system brought
again into full play, I have thought that noth-

ing was more likely to farther your lordship's views, than the publication of this little work, which concentrates, in a cheap and popular form, the high, true, orthodox, untainted legitimate principles; to which we owe so many violent though conscientious magistrates, and so many truckling though religious clergymen.

This work of my poor dear departed friend, and which I presume is an allegory, (as the facts that it relates are all unknown to me) will be found to convey a death-blow to all that pestilential stuff which is putting the holy alliance, and others, to such uneasiness; and which, though it is called Reform, evidently only means murder, rapes, upsetting of altars, carnage, house-breaking, and beheading of kings; which had deluged Europe with seas of blood, and has struck off so many taxes, places, sinecures, and pensions, from well-affected courtiers and orthodox rats. The great effects which I naturally anticipate from the publication of this allegory, will draw your lordship's attention to me; and I cannot imagine that you will do less than present me two neighbouring livings, valued each at £400 per annum; and I can assure you, that, though I was once a violent radical, and am now a Socinian, yet I will give up both politics and religion, for the sake of anything that you may have to give, or I to gain. The question of reform has been wisely settled on the continent, by the holy alliance; and, at present, the high price of corn, the facility of getting rents, and the *general prosperity of the kingdom*, (as the ministers term it, when praising one another) has lulled it here in England with equal facility; so that now is the time for government to make aggressions, and for adventurers to change their politics; and to become that sacred animal which is generally known by the name of "rat," and of which more may be said on another occasion. Amongst the rats, I am most anxious to be classed; and I do assure your lordship, that, when you have given me a living, I will become a furious and unjust magistrate, a persecutor of poachers, a punisher of untried prisoners, a member of the county Pitt club, a drinker of port wine, a sporting divine, a reader of John Bull, a reviler of methodists, an abuser of bible societies, an enemy to the catholics, a hater of popery, and, in one word, a sound legitimate both in politics and faith.

Your lordship must have observed that the deans, and doctors, and admirals, and bishops, and half-pay officers have of late years drawn all their notions on morals and politics, from that orthodox paper of ribaldry the "John Bull;" whose loyalty and bawdry are so well known; and of this excellent paper I would observe, that for the better instruction of the country gentlemen, it has abbreviated the study of religion in the short word — "*Cant;*" that, for the abstruse science of morals, it has substituted, "*Humbug;*" and for patriotism, "*Blarney.*" Now I, who am of the abbreviating school, wish to add another word of this expressive sort, particularly as it alludes to that species of vice which this little work treats of; — I mean, "sentiment, humanity, gentleness of disposition," &c. &c. which, in a monosyllable, I beg to term "*Rot;*" that is to say, a rotten thing, a refuse dung-hill, a vile lump of filth; so that with Cant, Humbug, Blarney, and Rot, we shall have four weapons by which we may throw ridicule upon all opponents; and by which piety, virtue, patriotism, and sentiment, may be laid prostrate before interested adventurers, whose sole object, as your lordship knows, is to laugh at all right feeling; and, having established vice as a system, keep that which depends on this system. When your lordship has perused this work, you will see how absurd and dangerous it is to indulge in that vile sort of sentiment, which has lately sprung up, and which would prevent country gentlemen from indulging in the noble and truly aristocratic amusement of "cruelty to animals." What can Mr. Martin mean by his idle paradoxes? Is it not as absurd to prevent cruelty to animals, as to endeavour to abolish the game laws? What can be more wicked? Must not the country gentlemen be encouraged? How can you persuade them to stay in the country, and set such good examples to the lower orders, (as we all know they do) if you do not allow them their ancient and hallowed amusements, of murdering fowls by thousands on the first of August; of badger-baiting; of the cock-pit; of dog-fights; and flogging their dogs every day, all winter through; of hare-hunting, and all the other little sanguinary delights, in which young 'squires take such pleasure, and for which they are so famed? What is a country gentleman worth, if he may not send poachers to the Bay? Are not our virtues all founded on these noble, gymnastic, athletic, gentlemanly amusements? Do we not, my lord, owe all our manly courage to the right of cruelty to animals? Are not our tall peasantry, our "country's pride," all trained up in vigour and magnanimity by bull-baiting, and dog-fights? Oh! my lord! sentiment will be the ruin of us; and though there is a sure majority in the house yet, some day or other I perceive that humanity will sap the foundation of these things; will abridge the country gentlemen of their pleasures, and thus bring down the crown, the mitre, and the law, in one common ruin, and "great will be the fall thereof!"

This allegory, however, will be some slight check to the mania of kindness to man and beast, which continually is goading the aristocracy, like a heavy collar on a sore neck. It will shew how foolish and wicked it is, to indulge in theories that may tend to so much mischief; and will prove, to your lordship's satisfaction, that the adage holds good with regard to animals; for if you give them an inch, they will take an ell; and there is no saying, what confusion and mischief may be brought of the kingdom, if the dangerous doctrines of humanity are preached to beasts in their present degraded situation; who, without any means of weighing well the truth, will of course receive with greediness the visionary tales of designing demagogues; and, believing all that is said, burst out at last into open and dreadful rebellion.

Depend upon it, my lord, humanity is as bad as patriotism. I cannot bear this fury for teaching and instructing, and improving *morally* the condition of our inferiors. He was no friend to legitimacy, that taught the learned pig; and nothing is so cruel, or so wicked, as to make the lower orders wiser than their betters.—A poor man, and a poodle-dog should never be taught to read; they are much happier in their present condition;—and a cow and a negro are infinitely more to be envied, than the well-taught and democratic peasantry of England, who would give their ears to be as well-fed, and as ignorant, as our West Indian slaves.

Your lordship knows that we all live for what we can get; that virtue and religion are not the object of our wishes; that the fees and delays of the law are more profitable than piety, and sentiment; and that we are never satisfied, till we have got as much as it is possible to receive. What then, I would ask, is the criterion of happiness, but plenty? Plenty makes man and beast contented; and I consider a satisfied jack-ass infinitely superior to a lord who has not yet got as much as he desires. But, once for all, I protest against all "cant, humbug, blarney, and rot." Your lordship and myself will not, I trust, acknowledge that stupid system of kindness to man and beast, that is deluging the world with its madness and its mischief; and I do hope, nay I feel confident, that we shall not be so far degraded, as to be termed philanthropists when we have descended into the grave.

The rage of the liberals and the radicals will be very great against this little work; and I have no doubt that it will be furiously reviewed in Edinburgh and Westminster, to throw an odium if possible on the memory of the author, who, however, is far beyond the reach of their mal-

ice; and who lived and died in the firm, un-
shaken principles, of thorough-paced, undevi-
ating legitimacy, for which he got much abuse,
and a good living, while he was alive; and who,
though perhaps he carried his notions somewhat too far, (being of the divine right school)
yet may be excused for his worthy prejudices,
when your lordship is informed that he was an
old bachelor, who never stirred from his college gates, except when he found it requisite to
appear amongst his parishioners, to raise his
tythes in exact proportion with their industry.

At present, it is requisite to conceal the
author's name; but if the public should favor
the production of my learned friend's genius,
and if it should be considered a useful remedy
for the evils against which it was written, I can
assure your lordship that there are other stories of this sort in readiness, equally useful, and
equally amusing. In short, this work may be
considered the first of a series; and, such as it
is, it is dedicated most humbly to your lordship; who I have no doubt will have the kindness to recommend it to the many under your
care, and by their means to the society for pro-
moting Christian knowledge, as a book of infi-

nite more importance and morality, than Robinson Crusoe, or Mrs. Trimmer's stories, so many thousands of which are printed for the lower orders, as a gilding to the pill of the XXXIX articles; which, I fear, sometimes stick in the throat, mixed up, as they generally are, with the doctrine of tythes.

Finally, my lord, allow me to say a word for myself: and to assure you, that, with the hopes of obtaining an excellent living, I am the humblest and most abject of your lordship's shoe-blacks; more ready to crawl, and lick your feet, than any clerical sycophant that ever before grovelled in the dust, or sold his conscience to a minister;—and though our order is famous for its political pliability, yet I do beg your lordship to consider me, if possible, still more slavish than usual; more ready to obey any commands that may be given me; more supple, more courteous, more docile, and more obedient, than any other in his majesty's dominions.

I have the honor to subscribe myself,
  My lord,
  Your lordship's thorough varlet,
  JOHN PIMPLICO.